T

A Brim

(Book 13)

By

April Fernsby

www.aprilfernsby.com

Front Cover by www.coverkicks.com[1]

Proofreading done by Paula Proofreader[2]

---

1. http://www.coverkicks.com

2. https://paulaproofreader.wixsite.com/home

Chapter One

"I can't go. Not to that place," Blythe said as she settled farther back in her armchair. "You'll have to go, Cassia. Take Stanley with you. Would you like more tea?"

"No, thank you. Three cups are more than enough for me." I glanced at my cat and familiar, Stanley, and asked him, "Do you need anything more to drink?"

He let out a chuckle and patted his stomach. "I'm already awash with milk. I don't think I could have another drop."

I gave my attention back to Blythe and said, "Where is this place you can't go to? And why can't you go there?"

She gave us a wide smile. "It's a delightful place. I'm afraid if I go there, I won't want to leave. You'll see what I mean when you visit. I'm not sure an investigation is needed at the moment, but we'll get more information when Mrs Tarblast arrives. She said she'll be here soon."

Stanley said, "I'm looking forward to having a new investigation, if it is one. We haven't had anything for a few weeks, have we, Cassia?"

"No," I agreed. "It's been suspiciously quiet here in Brimstone. It worries me when it's too quiet."

Blythe nodded. "I feel the same. I'm on edge most of the time, waiting for something terrible to happen." She let out a small laugh. "How did it come to this in our lovely town? Here we are, waiting for something awful to happen instead of appreciating the loveliness of this place. I need another drink." She clicked her fingers and a cup appeared in the air, no doubt full of extra-strong tea. I'd noticed Blythe was drinking a lot of strong tea lately. I suppose it was better than drinking wine or vodka.

I was a justice witch in the magical town of Brimstone, and Blythe was in charge of the town. She was three hundred years old but didn't look a day over forty, or even thirty on a good day, depending on how much magic she'd used on herself.

Stanley asked, "How's Mrs Tarblast getting on with her new role?"

Blythe shook her head in despair. "The power has gone straight to her head. I'm sure that little gnome seems taller every time I see her. Or maybe it's the new way she carries herself. Still, at least it keeps her on the right side of the law." She paused and considered her words. "Most of the time anyway. I'm having to turn a blind eye to some of the plants and flowers she brings back from other towns. She claims she has to keep doing it to not arouse suspicion. She argues that she has to carry on as normal. I'll be honest, I'm still not entirely sure where her loyalties lie."

There was a knock at the front door and Blythe called out, "Come in. It's open!"

A few seconds later, a gnome in a red dress with white polka dots bustled in and gave us a welcoming wave. She had her usual wicker basket slung over her arm.

Stanley waved his paw and said, "Hello Mrs Tarblast. You look well. How are you?"

"I'm rushed off my feet, but I can't complain, Stanley. It's not in my nature." She walked over to a little stool which had been placed next to the sofa. Using the stool, she climbed on the sofa and settled herself down next to me, basket at her side.

She asked, "Is there any tea going? My throat is so parched I can barely talk."

Blythe clicked her fingers in Mrs Tarblast's direction and a cup appeared. Blythe said dryly, "Here you are. We wouldn't want you to lose your voice, would we?"

Mrs Tarblast chuckled. "There'll be no chance of that if you keep supplying me with tea. I suppose a biscuit is beyond your magical capabilities?"

Blythe shook her head at the gnome. "You literally do take the biscuit, Mrs Tarblast." She waved her fingers and a plate appeared on the table in front of the gnome. It was piled high with a variety of biscuits. Blythe said, "Can we get down to business now? Or would you like a full roast dinner? Or perhaps an ice cream sundae?"

Mrs Tarblast picked a biscuit up and dumped it in her tea. "There's no need for sarcasm. Is that how you talk to a valued colleague?"

Blythe looked at me and raised her eyebrows in exasperation.

I said to Mrs Tarblast, "How are you getting on in your intelligence agent role? I hope it's not too much work for you."

She munched on the biscuit before answering. "It's not too much for me. I felt a bit weird about it at first, as if I was being a sneak. But then I reckoned I was the best one for this job. I'm helping you witches by going to places you couldn't without standing out like sore thumbs. I don't know why you didn't give me this job before."

Blythe clamped her lips together to stop herself from speaking. I couldn't help but smile at Mrs Tarblast's righteous expression. As annoying as she was, she was excellent at picking up important bits of information that we witches might not come across. I think it was either by luck or just plain nosiness that she found things out.

Blythe said, "Have you got something to tell us or not? Or is this a ploy to come here and eat me out of biscuits?"

"You are so impatient. Hang on a mo." Mrs Tarblast brushed a few crumbs from her dress, took a sip of tea and put her cup down. She reached into her basket and pulled something out. "If we're starting our official meeting, I need to dress the part."

We watched in amazement as she pulled on a jacket which was white with red polka dots. She smoothed down the collar and straightened the sleeves. With a satisfied smile, she explained, "This is my official intelligence agent jacket. Quite snazzy, don't you think? I made it myself."

Stanley nodded. "You look amazing. Really professional."

"Thank you. That's the look I was going for." She clasped her hands together. "Right. Let's get this meeting started. Blythe, do you need to write anything down for official purposes?"

"No, I think we'll be able to remember everything you say." There was a hint of amusement in Blythe's voice.

"Okay. Then I'll begin. Cassia, have you heard of the Mirella Retirement Village?"

I shook my head. "Has there been a murder there?"

Mrs Tarblast tutted. "Why do you always assume there's been a murder? You've got death on your mind." She paused for thought. "Although, you might be right in this case. It might lead to murder. But that's for you to investigate. If you're quick enough, you might stop something terrible happening."

Blythe held one hand up. "Mrs Tarblast, you're going off at a tangent. Just give us the facts."

Mrs Tarblast bristled somewhat but continued. "Mirella Retirement Village is named after a particular flower which only grows in that area. I've never seen it growing anywhere else, not on my travels anyway. It's called Mirella Phlox, and it's a lovely shade of blue. I use it quite often in my lotions and potions. It has amazing healing abilities. The best place to harvest those flowers is behind certain homes in the village. Those homes are owned by witches. And I think those witches are in trouble."

Chapter Two

"Witches?" Stanley sat up straighter. "Don't tell me a witch is about to be murdered."

Mrs Tarblast gave him a gentle look. "I don't know that anyone is about to be murdered. Let me explain. In the retirement village, there's one witch who has a huge patch of Mirella Phlox in her garden. She's called Brigid Sangrey."

"Brigid Sangrey?" Blythe repeated. "I've seen her a few times at witch conferences. I don't know much about her, though."

Mrs Tarblast continued. "Brigid and I have an understanding about those flowers. I let her know I'm on my way to her house, and she stands at the kitchen window waiting for me. When I arrive, I go into the back garden and help myself to the flowers. She rushes out of her house and chases me around the garden. It's a great game."

I frowned. "It doesn't sound like a great game to me. It sounds like you're stealing her flowers, and then she's chasing you off her property."

Mrs Tarblast nodded. "It does sound that way, but there's more than enough flowers in Brigid's back garden. I'm doing her a favour by taking some of them away. And she does love chasing me around the garden. She says it's good exercise. But she's getting on a bit, and I have to slow down sometimes to give her a fighting chance to catch me. When she does catch me, we go and sit down and have a little chat. I even give her some of the lotions I've made from the flowers. She doesn't like to rely on magic all the time when she needs to treat her aches and pains. And like I said, those flowers have great healing powers."

"I'm confused," Stanley admitted. "Are you sure she's not angry at you for stealing her flowers?"

"Brigid loves our meetings. She says it adds excitement to her week. To be honest, I think she's a bit bored at that retirement village. Sometimes, if she's not at the kitchen window looking out for me, I'll go and knock on the door and let her know I'm there. I've found her having a nap more than once. But I wake her up, and she's always pleased to see me." She frowned at the table in front of her, but didn't say anything.

Sensing we were getting closer to the problem, I asked, "Is there something wrong with Brigid? Is that why you're here now in your official capacity?"

Mrs Tarblast sighed and gave me a direct look. "Brigid has gone missing. I called on her at the beginning of last week as my flower supplies were running low, but she never appeared at the kitchen window. I knocked on the door and peeped through the windows, but I couldn't see her anywhere. She's got two witch friends who live on either side of her. They know about our little chasing game. I called on them too, but they were not at home either. I thought maybe they'd gone on holiday or something, not that they need a holiday living at that retirement village, but you never know."

Blythe enquired, "Did you ask around the village to see if anyone knew where they were?"

"I did. Nobody knows where they might have gone. I even asked that grumpy creature who's in charge of the upkeep of the village. But he didn't know where they'd gone. Not that he'd tell me if he did know. Miserable piece, he is. Creg; that's his name." A worried look came into her eyes. "Something's niggling me about their disappearance. I didn't think they'd leave the village without telling me, certainly not Brigid. So I called again at the village yesterday, but still, they weren't there. Something doesn't feel right in that village. It's changed. And not for the good. The atmosphere made the hairs on my arms and legs stand up."

I said, "Do you want Stanley and me to investigate? Maybe talk to the residents?"

Mrs Tarblast nodded. "I know how nosy you are, no offence. And Stanley has a way about him which gets everyone talking. You might want to start with Brigid's grandson. He calls on her every week. He's called Trent. He's a skinny little thing. A strong gust would knock him over. He was at Brigid's house yesterday. I asked him if he knew where his grandma had gone. But he was just as confused as me. And worried too. He said his grandma would never leave the village without telling him. Cassia, it would be a good idea if you went to the retirement village as soon as possible. Trent thinks he can deal with his grandma's disappearance on his own."

"Why does he think that?" I asked

"Because he's been receiving witch training from Brigid. As far as I know, he's only been taught a few spells. But he seems to think that's enough to make him an expert in magical matters. I'm afraid something terrible will happen to him if he starts poking his nose where it doesn't belong." She looked over at Blythe. "Is it okay if I ask Cassia and Stanley to go to the village? Is this the sort of problem you wanted me to look out for?"

I was surprised at the worry in the gnome's voice. She must be really concerned about the missing witches.

Blythe gave her a kind look. "This is exactly the kind of situation we need to know about. Thank you for telling us."

Mrs Tarblast sat up a bit straighter. "You are welcome."

Blythe addressed me, "The village is just within the boundaries of Brimstone, so I do have authority to send you there. If anyone questions you, tell them I sent you."

"I will." I turned to Stanley and said, "It looks like we've got a new investigation. Are you ready to make a start?"

He leapt off the sofa and said, "Always. We'll find out what's happened to those missing witches."

Blythe put her cup down and said solemnly, "Cassia, make sure you come back to Brimstone. Even though you're not old enough to retire, once you get to Mirella Retirement Village, you might never want to leave."

Chapter 3

Blythe told us where to find Mirella Retirement Village. And Mrs Tarblast gave us details on where the witches lived in the village.

Blythe added, "Come back here if you need our help with anything. And, of course, if there's a murder or two, let me know."

"I will," I replied. "But I hope it doesn't come to that."

She nodded. "Me too, but you never know these days. Have a safe flight."

We said goodbye and were soon airborne on my broomstick.

From the front of the broomstick, Stanley looked over his shoulder and said, "What do you think this retirement village will look like? I've seen those adverts on the TV about villages for the elderly. They're lovely places with lots of grey-haired people walking around. Do you think it'll be anything like that?"

"Perhaps. Maybe they'll have gentle activities for the residents, like golf or swimming. Or painting classes by a river. I imagine they'll want a lot of peace and quiet. And they'll need to have doctors nearby in case they get ill."

Stanley continued, "What if they have frozen food brought right to their door? That would be so good, wouldn't it? It would save them the trouble of cooking. Have you seen that man on the TV who delivers frozen food to the elderly? He even puts the meals in customers' freezers. And he's always smiling. Do you think they'll have deliveries like that?"

I shrugged. "They might have their own restaurants or cafes. I haven't really given retirement villages much thought."

"If they do have restaurants and cafes, they would have to serve food which is easy on the digestion. Don't older people get lots of stomach upsets if they eat spicy food? That's what happens to your gran. But she still eats those curries you make her."

I smiled. "Yes, but you know what Gran's like. She loves her spicy food. And don't forget she can use magic on herself to get rid of her indigestion. I wonder why Blythe said we wouldn't want to leave once we saw what the village was like?"

"We'll soon find out. I'm excited to start our new investigation, aren't you? Looking for missing witches will make a change from trying to find a murderer."

I didn't answer. Murder never seemed to be far away from us lately. And missing witches could lead to murdered witches.

We flew on in silence for the next twenty minutes until Mirella Retirement Village came into view. It was a huge area, and from our position up high we could see how the village was separated into different parts. One area, in particular, caught my attention.

Stanley noticed it too because he waved his paw excitedly and said, "Can you see that? Is that an amusement park? Right in the middle of the retirement village? That can't be right, can it? Have we gone the wrong way?"

"Not according to Blythe's directions. Let's have a closer look."

We flew closer to the area which looked more like a theme park than a retirement village. I took in the fast-spinning rides, roller coasters, log flumes and other high-adrenaline rides.

Screams of joy and fear filled the air along with the aroma of hot food. The rides were packed with creatures of many species, all beaming and laughing.

Stanley looked my way and gave me a quizzical look. "We must be in the wrong place. Elderly creatures can't go on those rides. They might pull a muscle or break a bone. Do you think they've been forced to go on the rides against their will?"

"Not by the looks on their faces. They seem to be having a great time." I turned the broomstick to the left. "Let's see what the rest of the village looks like from up here."

We flew over to the next part of the village which was a large forest area. I caught glimpses of small meadows between the trees. Wooden walkways connected most of the trees, and I could see many wooden houses nestled in the branches of the trees. Various creatures were walking along the tree walkways and down in the meadows. Some of them were gently jogging. Some creatures were sprinting at impressive speeds. I even witnessed residents whizzing along zip lines between the trees.

Stanley observed the area and said, "This looks like an outdoor boot camp. You can't have elderly creatures climbing up to those tree houses. Their wobbly legs might give way before they reach the top. And who's making those residents run so fast? It's not right. Is this actually a prison camp? Is that why Blythe didn't want to come here? It's too dangerous." He shook his head. "I don't understand this at all."

"They seem happy enough," I pointed out. "We should land and have a good look around. We'll start talking to beings too. Let's start with the one who's in charge of the upkeep of the village. Didn't Mrs Tarblast say he's called Creg?"

"Didn't she say he was grumpy too?" Stanley chuckled. "But he could be grumpy because he was talking to Mrs Tarblast. She does bring out the bad-tempered side of creatures sometimes. Not me, though. I like her."

We flew away from the forest area and over to the edge of the village. According to Mrs Tarblast's instructions, Creg lived in a wooden hut at the entrance of the village. I spotted a solitary hut and headed towards it.

We landed next to the hut and dismounted. A second later, the door was flung open and a tall, thick-set creature stormed out. His face was full of fury. Stanley and I took an involuntary step back. I had no idea what kind of a creature he was. His face was elongated and covered in warts and bumps. Clumps of dark hairs sprouted out of every one of those lumps and bumps. He was wearing a dark brown jumper which had holes everywhere. Thick hairs poked through the various holes, which made me feel a bit queasy. It wasn't just his appearance which was unsettling. There was a terrible odour coming from him. A mixture of rotten fish, decaying vegetables, and manure from goodness knows what creature. The stink washed over us in waves.

With some effort, I managed to stop myself gagging. I cast a quick glance at Stanley and could see how he was struggling not to gag too.

The creature snapped, "What do you want? Why haven't you come through the gate?" He glowered at my broomstick. "Who gave you permission to land?"

The sour smell from his breath made my eyes water, and it took all my willpower to stand my ground. I wondered if I could discreetly cast a spell on Stanley and me to protect our noses. But the creature was staring at me so intently that I was afraid to move a muscle.

As politely as I could, I said, "Hello, I'm Cassia Winter, and this is Stanley."

Stanley waved his paw and said, "Hello." He subtly put his paw in front of his nose.

I continued, "Are you Creg?"

His eyes narrowed in suspicion causing them to nearly disappear under his bushy eyebrows. "What's it got to do with you who I am?" He picked something from his ear, looked at it and flicked it away.

Ignoring his rudeness, I went on, "We've come from Brimstone to investigate the disappearance of some residents here. I believe you spoke to Mrs Tarblast about them."

He spat on the ground, narrowly missing my feet. "That nosy gnome. What's she been saying about me? I wouldn't listen to a word she says. Sneaking in here whenever she feels like it. I've a good mind to tell the owner to start charging her."

"Is it true some of your residents have gone missing? Three witches?"

He shrugged. "Who knows? Who cares? What's it got to do with you anyway?"

I lifted my chin slightly. "I'm concerned about their disappearance. Stanley and I are going to find out where they've gone." Something about the dismissive look on his face compelled me to add, "Have you got a problem with that?"

"What if I have? Who do I complain to?"

"You can complain to Blythe in Brimstone. She gave us permission to look into the witches' disappearance. When did you last see them?"

He rummaged about in his ear again. "I can't remember. I don't know who's here and who's not. It's none of my business. As long as they don't make too much mess, that's all I'm bothered about."

I could see we were getting nowhere with him, and his foul scent was increasing by the second. I said, "We're going to have a look around the village and speak to the residents."

"Do what you want. I couldn't care less." He pulled something from his ear, and to my disgust, he put it in his mouth. "Don't get in my way. Don't damage anything. If you're here for more than three hours, you'll have to pay a visitor's fee. Shift. I've got work to do. Some hairy werewolf has bunged up his shower again." He made a move forward which caused me and Stanley to step to the side swiftly.

"Before you go," I said, "do you have any maps of the village?"

He gave us a filthy look before bending down and drawing some circles in the dirt. He jabbed his finger at the circles. "That's where the residents live. That's The Forest Zone. That's The Quiet Zone. Over there is The Fun Zone. And that bit in the middle is the clubhouse. Got it?" Before we could answer, he rubbed the diagram out with his mud-encrusted boot. He spat on the ground once more before striding away.

Stanley looked at me and said, "Charming."

"Not to worry. We can always nip up to the sky to get our bearings if we have to."

Stanley nodded. "Where shall we begin?"

"We should start with Brigid's home. If she has gone on holiday, perhaps we'll find evidence of that." I gave him a hopeless look. "I'm not sure what that evidence would be as we've never been to her home before, but it's the best place to start."

Stanley nodded. "We have to begin somewhere. Cassia, have you seen the little flowers that are dotted around? Do you think they're the Mirella Phlox Mrs Tarblast told us about?"

I looked towards a little patch of flowers at his side. The flowers were small and looked like daisies. The blue petals were the colour of the sky on a clear day. Tiny flecks of gold and silver were dotted throughout the petals, catching the sunlight.

Stanley padded over to the nearest patch and gave it a quick sniff. "I don't know what this smell is, but it's lovely." He looked at me and gave me a grin. "They smell much better than Creg. He did whiff a bit, didn't he?"

"More than a bit," I said with a smile. "According to that diagram he drew, the area where everyone lives is just down this path here."

We walked down the path and towards the residential area. The little blue flowers were dotted at many intervals along the path. The gold and silver flecks continued to catch the sun's rays making them look like precious gems.

We soon arrived at the residential area and saw a selection of buildings. Two-storey apartment buildings were mixed in with detached bungalows. Log cabins were placed next to simple huts. Mrs Tarblast had told us Brigid lived in one of the cottages to the left. And I recalled that her witch friends lived on either side of her.

As we headed that way, the number of blue flowers increased along the path until they became a blue carpet. They grew thicker in the garden of the middle cottage. We walked towards it. A wooden plaque on the wall next to the door confirmed Brigid Sangrey lived there.

I pointed the name out to Stanley and said, "We're at the right place."

Stanley looked around. "I wonder why there are so many flowers here?"

I knocked on the door firmly and waited for an answer. No one came to the door. I knocked a few more times to be on the safe side, and then tried the handle. The door opened.

Stanley and I hesitated. He asked, "Are we going inside?"

"Yes. We can't stand on the doorstep all day." I kept a firm hold on my broomstick in case I needed to use it as a weapon. Something about an empty house with an unlocked door unsettled me.

I stepped into the house with Stanley right behind me.

Before I could take in my surroundings, someone leapt out of the shadows and knocked me to the ground.

Chapter 4

I lay on the ground, too stunned to speak. I heard someone shouting, "Who are you? What are you doing here?"

Then I heard Stanley yelling, "Get away from Cassia right now! Don't make me hurt you!"

I looked up at the person who had been shouting at me and saw a young man with a bright red face. He was wearing a jumper which was far too large for him. A yellow duster was being waved from his skinny hand in my direction. Stanley had his paws around the man's leg as if trying to drag him away from me.

The man continued to shout, "How dare you break into Grandma's house?"

I swiftly got to my feet and said, "We didn't break in. The front door was unlocked. Are you Trent? The grandson of Bridget Sangrey?"

He gave me a suspicious look. "I might be." He flapped the duster at me. "And if I am, how do you know my name? And what are you doing here? And can you tell your pet to get off my leg?"

Stanley looked at me questioningly and I gave him a nod. He took his paws away and came to my side.

I said, "I'm Cassia Winter, and this is Stanley. We've come from Brimstone to investigate the disappearance of your grandma. I'm assuming you are Trent, aren't you?"

He lowered the duster a fraction. "I am. I know about Brimstone, Grandma told me about it. I don't understand what you're doing here, though. And how do you know Grandma is missing?"

Stanley answered, "Mrs Tarblast told us. She's a gnome who lives in Brimstone. She helps us now and again. Do you know her?"

Trent ignored Stanley's question. He said loudly, "I'm dealing with Grandma's disappearance. There's no need for you to be here." He looked at the duster in his hand as if surprised to see it there. "I'm keeping her house clean until I find out where she's gone. I don't need any help finding Grandma. You can go now."

I said firmly, "We're not going anywhere. Trent, do you know who Blythe is? She lives in Brimstone."

Trent nodded. "Isn't she in charge or something?"

"She is," I confirmed. "She's concerned about your grandma and the other witches. She's asked Stanley and me to find out where they are."

Trent shoved the duster in his pocket. "I don't need your help. I've got everything under control. Grandma would want me to find her, not some stranger. I can use magic to find her. I know five spells." He gave me a defiant look.

Stanley said gently, "Cassia has been training as a witch for a while now. She knows lots of spells. She's very good. I'm certain she'll find your grandma soon."

Once again, Trent ignored Stanley's comments and said to me, "You can help me. But don't get in my way. And you have to do what I say."

I said firmly, "Trent, I'm sorry your grandma has gone missing, but I am going to deal with this investigation with Stanley's help. I'm going to decide what happens next, and who we talk to. You can help by telling us what you know, starting with when you last saw your grandma."

"What if I don't want to tell you?" He lifted his chin.

"Then you will be hindering our investigation, but I hope it won't come to that. Do you want to find your grandma and the other witches? Will you help us?"

His chin dropped. "I suppose I could help you a bit. What do you want to know?"

"When did you last see your grandma, and where?" I began.

"It was about two weeks ago. I come here for magic lessons with Grandma, but I'm not getting very far with them." He smiled a little. "She does go on a bit. She likes to tell stories about all the things she's done in the past. I love listening to her, but I sometimes wish she'd teach me magic instead of going on and on about her life. I want to be a powerful witch just like her, and it would happen more quickly if she concentrated on me and not herself."

Was it my imagination or was there a hint of bitterness in his voice?

I asked, "Where did you meet her for your magic lessons? Was it in here?"

He nodded. "Yeah, but sometimes I would find her in the forest. She's got a special area where she sits. She goes there a lot to tell the other oldies about her adventures. They love listening to her, and Grandma loves talking to them. Before you ask, I've asked the oldies about Grandma, but no one knows where she's gone. So, you don't need to talk to them."

"I'll decide that for myself," I told him sternly. "When did you last see the other witches?" I recalled the names Mrs Tarblast had given us. "Edie Calarook and Avalon Tempest?"

Trent waved his hand in one direction and said, "Edie lives at that side of Grandma." He pointed the opposite way. "Avalon lives that way. I haven't seen them for days. I didn't even know they'd gone missing till I started looking for Grandma. I wanted to ask them where she'd gone, but they weren't in."

Stanley asked, "Is this the first time your grandma has left without letting you know?"

Without looking at Stanley, Trent replied, "She's never gone missing before. Ever. And if she did have to leave suddenly, she would have left me a note." His voice caught in his throat. "This is not like her at all. She'd never leave without telling me. Never." Tears came to his eyes and he quickly looked away.

My tone was gentle as I asked, "Who did your grandma talk to in the village? Was she well-liked? Did she have any enemies?"

Anger infused Trent's face. "Enemies? Of course she didn't have any enemies! Grandma is wonderful. Everyone loves her. Why are you asking that?" His eyes narrowed. "Do you think something terrible has happened to her? Is that why you're really here?"

"We have to consider all possibilities," I replied diplomatically. "Do you know your way around this village? Could you show us around?"

"I suppose I can do that. But I don't know why you think she might have enemies. That's just stupid. Follow me." He turned around and headed out of the door.

I lowered myself and whispered to Stanley, "Well? What do you think about Trent?"

"I don't know what to think, but I suspect he knows more than he's letting on."

"I agree. We'll get the truth from him eventually." I stroked Stanley's head. "I don't like how he keeps ignoring you."

Stanley gave me a small smile. "Perhaps he doesn't like cats."

"Then he's a fool." I straightened up and followed Trent. Stanley padded behind me.

We had to jog to catch up with Trent. When we caught up with him, he surprised me by asking, "Do you want to see what Grandma looks like? And the other witches?"

"Have you got photographs of them?" I asked.

His smile was smug. "Something better than that. You'll see." He strode ahead and we had to jog again to keep up with him.

We came to a smooth path made of stones. Trent advised, "This path leads to the clubhouse. That's where everyone meets." He pointed to a small statue at the side of the path. "Each resident has a statue along this path. It was Grandma's idea to have these statues. She said everyone would then know who lives here. When someone leaves, their statue disappears."

I looked at the imp-shaped figure at my side. It was made of a darker stone than the path. The one next to it was a fairy.

I asked, "Are these all life-sized?"

Trent nodded as he strode along. "Yes. Grandma and the other witches have their statues at the end of the path right next to the clubhouse. Where they belong."

"Where they belong?" I repeated. "Why do you say that?"

Trent looked over his shoulder at me and gave me a look as if it were obvious. "It's because Grandma is the most important resident here. She's the most powerful, so she should go at the front."

I shared a look with Stanley as we walked along with the path. The stone figures at our sides changed to represent different creatures. If I lived here and had to pass the statue of a witch who thought herself more important than me, I wouldn't like it one little bit. I began to suspect Brigid and the other witches had enemies who Trent didn't know about. Or perhaps he did know about them but didn't want to tell us.

The path led us to a large wooden building which had a veranda along its front. Several creatures were in rocking chairs on the veranda and watching our approach with interest.

As we got closer to the building, Trent came to a sudden stop and raised his hands to his face in horror. "No," he mumbled. "No. No."

"What's wrong?" I asked. I looked closer at the statues he was staring at. They looked more like wizards than witches to me.

Trent clenched his hands into fists. "The wizards! They've moved Grandma's statue and put theirs here instead! How dare they?" His eyes were full of hate as he glowered at the three wizards in front of him.

A sudden fear came to me. "Trent, if your grandma's statue isn't here, does that mean something has happened to her?"

Chapter 5

Trent uncurled his fists and looked along the line. In a flat voice, he said, "Grandma's statue is still here. Look." He pointed to a large figure. "The one next to her is Edie, and Avalon is next along. The evil wizards must have moved them."

I looked at the figure of his grandma and she immediately reminded me of someone who lived on Gran's street, Mrs Burnshaw. Mrs Burnshaw was a large and robust woman, full of self-importance and loud opinions. Whenever she walked down the street, she would walk right in the middle of it so that anyone coming her way was forced to move to the left or right. She would barge into people as if they weren't there. Brigid Sangrey had that same defiant look on her face.

Stanley noted, "She's holding a book in her hand. Trent, do you know what that book is?"

Trent was sending disgusted looks at the wizard and didn't hear Stanley's question. Or he was choosing to ignore my cat.

I said loudly, "Trent! What's the book?"

Trent tore his attention away from the wizard figures and explained, "It's Grandma's spellbook. She's had it since she was a girl. It's got all her important spells inside. And it's full of her stories too. She never lets it out of her sight."

"Have you ever seen inside it?" Stanley asked.

Trent turned slightly away from Stanley and said to me, "Grandma doesn't let anyone look inside it, let alone touch it."

His attitude towards Stanley was really starting to get on my nerves now, but I pushed my annoyance to one side. I asked him, "Have you checked your grandma's house to see if the book is there?"

He frowned. "I never thought to look for it. Why would I?"

There was no way to be diplomatic about this. I explained, "If the spellbook has gone, then your grandma could have left this village of her own accord. But if it's still in her house, she might have been taken against her will."

Stanley piped up, "If the book has gone it could also mean someone has stolen it. Trent, do you know who would want that book?"

Trent gave a shrug as his answer, his gaze firmly away from Stanley.

My irritation with him increased, so I moved along the line to look at the other figures.

Edie was the complete opposite of Brigid. She was small and meek looking. Her shoulders were bowed and her head dipped as if she was embarrassed to be there. Whoever made these statues had done an amazing job of catching someone's personality. I picked Stanley up so he could have a closer look at Edie.

Stanley must have noticed the same thing as me because he said to Trent, "Who made these statues?"

Trent looked at the ground and rolled a pebble along with the toe of his shoe. He muttered, "Grandma did."

We waited for him to expand on that, but he seemed more interested in the pebbles at his feet.

I moved down the line and examined the figure of Avalon. She was different from the other witches. She was wearing a short, form-fitting dress which skimmed her knees. Her hands were on her hips, and her face tipped skywards with an expression of utter joy in her eyes. I felt like she was going to starting laughing and dancing at any second.

Stanley said to me, "She looks like fun." He cast me a nervous glance. "Can you ask Trent what she was like? I don't think he likes talking to me."

"I don't think he does either, but that's his problem, not ours. You ask him, Stanley." I walked over to Trent and positioned myself so that Stanley was right in front of him.

Stanley cleared his throat and asked, "What do you know about Edie and Avalon? What was their relationship with your grandma like?"

Trent addressed his answers to the ground. "Edie was very quiet, but observant too. If you know what I mean."

I said loudly, "No, we don't know what you mean. Could you look our way when you're talking to us, please? What do you mean by your last remarks?"

Trent looked directly at me, his cheeks infused with colour. He explained, "Her eyes were always taking everything in, darting left and right as if she didn't want to miss anything. But she didn't speak much. She was more of a listener than a talker. She spent a lot of time in the meditation centre over that way." He nodded to the right.

"And what about this other witch, Avalon?" Stanley asked. "What is she like?"

Looking at me, Trent replied, "She's not like Edie at all. Very loud and outgoing. She spent most of her time in The Fun Zone. She loves mixing with others. Grandma didn't always approve of her behaviour and the company she kept, but Avalon would laugh at her and call her old-fashioned."

"Did they ever fall out about that?" I asked.

He gave a one-shoulder shrug. "I don't know. But I do know Avalon had been married fifteen times."

"Fifteen times!" Stanley and I exclaimed at the same time.

"Yeah, she likes getting married. I think some of her ex-husbands are living in this village somewhere."

"Really?" I said. "Do you know who they are? I would like to talk to them."

He gave me that shrug again. "I don't know. What have her ex-husbands got to do with my grandma?"

"We need as much information as possible about all the witches." I pointed out, "It isn't just your grandma who has gone missing."

Trent let out a sigh. "I suppose you're right, but can't we concentrate on finding Grandma first? Once we do that, I bet she'll know where the other witches are." He turned his head to look at the wizards again. "You should start with them. They're evil. And they don't like witches."

"I'll speak to them in due course," I informed him.

He snorted in derision. "I don't know why you don't just get on with it instead of asking me lots of useless questions. You're not much of a witch, are you? I thought you'd have everything sorted out by now using magic and spells."

Stanley cried out, "Hey! Don't you talk to Cassia like that."

Trent threw Stanley a look full of disgust.

That was the last straw.

I gave Trent a direct look and demanded, "What's your problem with Stanley?"

Chapter 6

Trent sneered and said, "Cats are wicked. Sneaky and evil. They shouldn't be allowed anywhere near a witch. Grandma never had a cat in her house. Neither did the other witches. Cats are horrible, I hate them."

Anger rose inside me but I kept hold of my temper. I pulled Stanley closer and said as calmly as I could, "Why do you think that?"

"Grandma said you can't trust them. They're selfish creatures. They don't care about anyone but themselves. They're nothing but trouble." Hate blazed in his eyes as he looked at Stanley. "She was right. Your cat keeps asking questions that have nothing to do with him. Who does he think he is anyway? You're the witch, not him. He should clear off; he's not welcome here."

My anger was making me tremble. Before I could give Trent a piece of my mind, Stanley said quietly, "Perhaps I should go back to Brimstone, Cassia. I don't want to get in the way of your investigation." He jumped out of my arms and looked up at me. Even though he was trying not to be upset at Trent's harsh words, his little chin wobbled as he bravely said, "I'll make my own way back. You don't have to worry about me."

Trent jabbed his finger at the path. "That's the way to the exit. Hurry up. And don't come back."

"Not another word!" I shouted at Trent. I raised a hand at him. "Not one more word about Stanley. He's the most courageous creature you would ever have the fortune to meet. He is loyal and intelligent, and I would never investigate a case without him at my side." I paused to take a breath to calm myself down.

Trent looked as if he were about to argue with me, but I didn't give him the opportunity. I carried on, "I don't know why you and your grandma hate cats, and I don't care. Stanley is more important to me in this investigation than you are, so you're the one who can clear off." I looked down at Stanley. "You are going nowhere, my dear friend. I need you by my side."

Trent yelled, "You can't tell me what to do! It's my grandma who's gone missing. It's up to me to find her."

I lowered my hand. "No, Trent, it's up to Stanley and me. You can leave."

I was surprised to see tears come to Trent's eyes. He looked at the ground and mumbled, "But I have to find her. She'd want me to find her."

For a moment, I could sense his sadness, but that didn't excuse his cruelty towards Stanley. I relented somewhat and said, "You may help, but only if your attitude towards Stanley changes. And it changes right now."

Trent didn't get the chance to speak because the aromatic keeper of the grounds, Creg, appeared from the side of the clubhouse. He marched over to us, took one look at the line of statues and yelled, "What have you done? Who said you could move them?"

His stench hit me right in the face causing me to waver on my feet.

Trent held his hands up in defence and said, "We didn't move them! It's those wizards. They must have done it."

Creg continued shouting, this time at Trent. "You did it! Don't deny it."

"I didn't! Why would I? I liked Grandma being at the front of the line where she belongs. It wasn't me!"

"Pah!" Creg retaliated. "You moved them because you argued with your grandma a while back. I heard you."

The colour vanished from Trent's face and he quickly glanced my way before looking back at Creg. "You don't know what you're talking about. I would never argue with Grandma. You're lying."

"Don't you talk to me like that. Don't forget you're a visitor here and I can throw you out. I heard you shouting at your grandma. Telling her to retire and give you her spellbook."

Trent cried out, "You liar! Leave me alone!" He spun around and stormed away from us.

Once he'd gone, I said to Creg, "What exactly did you hear?"

"I've told you all that I know." He scratched at a large boil on his chin. "Did you move these statues?"

"No."

He gave me a look of disbelief and continued to pick at his boil which made my stomach heave in revulsion. "I'll be keeping an eye on you," he said before walking away. His odour stayed right where it was.

I made a mental note to talk to him again later, but I'd cast a spell on Stanley and me first to protect us from his smell.

I said to Stanley, "Don't listen to a word Trent says about cats. He doesn't know how wonderful you are. Not yet."

Stanley let out a small laugh. "It doesn't matter. Not everyone is going to like me. What shall we do now? Do you want to go after Creg? I think his smell has got worse since we last spoke to him."

"I think so too. But I want to speak to Trent again. I want to know more about this argument he had with his grandma. I knew he was keeping something from us. Let's catch up with him."

Before we left the statues, I decided to take a couple of photos using my phone. I made sure I got pictures of the witches and the wizards. When that was done, Stanley and I set off after Trent at a jog which is not my favourite way to travel.

I spotted Trent ahead and called out, "Trent! Wait!"

He looked over his shoulder, saw us and broke into a sprint.

"Oh no you don't." I sent an immobilizing spell his way, and a few seconds later he was hovering in mid-stride above the ground.

Once Stanley and I reached him, I released him from the spell but made sure my arm was firmly on his shoulder to prevent him running off.

As he came out of the spell I said firmly, "You've got some explaining to do."

"Let me go!" He tried to wriggle away, but my grip intensified.

"Was Creg right about the argument you had with your grandma?" I asked.

Trent nodded. "It wasn't as bad as he made out. I was getting fed up with Grandma being so slow at teaching me magic. She kept going on and on about all the adventures she'd been on. And I got sick of listening to them. How was I going to have adventures of my own if she never taught me all the spells I needed? But I didn't do anything to her, if that's what you're thinking. I didn't make her disappear. I wouldn't even know how to."

I gave him a brisk nod, not sure if I believed him. "We're going back to Brigid's house to look for her spellbook. Have you any idea where she kept it?"

"No. Let me go." He wriggled again.

I released him, picked Stanley up and headed towards Brigid's house not caring if Trent followed us or not.

Once in Brigid's house, I didn't want to waste time by searching every nook and cranny, so I used a locating spell to find her book. It led us upstairs and into her bedroom. I heard Trent shouting at me and telling me not to go into her room. I ignored him.

I soon found the spellbook. It was in her bedside cabinet. I reached out for it.

I jumped as Trent called out from right behind me, "Don't touch it!"

Chapter 7

My hand hovered over the book. I asked Trent, "Why shouldn't I touch it?"

"Grandma could have put some protective magic on it," he explained. He took a step closer to the book. "And if she has, I don't think it would work on me, not with me being her grandson. I'd better take it." He took another step.

I put my hand on his chest. "Stay right where you are. If there's magic on this book, I know how to reveal it. And I know how to get rid of it."

"But I—"

"But nothing," I cut him off. "Stand back." I gave him a gentle push. He moved back with a glower on his face. He was good at glowering.

I used a magic revealing spell on the book, but no pale blue light of magic appeared. That could mean there wasn't a spell, or that Brigid had cast a strong spell which couldn't be detected.

Either way, I couldn't leave the book where it was. I grimaced and reached out again, preparing myself for any pain from a protective spell.

Thankfully, there wasn't any. I picked the book up and examined it. It was bound in battered black leather. The pages were bulky and misshapen. I carefully opened the book and began to look through it. I was suddenly aware of Trent breathing over my shoulder.

"Back away," I said. "Don't you know the meaning of personal space?"

"Eh? What do you mean? Let me have a look at that book."

"No. I'm looking at it." I closed the book and gave him a pointed look until he backed up. Then I opened the book again. The pages were full of peculiar-looking symbols and scribblings. If these were words, I didn't recognise them whatsoever.

I held the book out to Trent and asked him, "Do you recognise these words?"

His scrunched-up face gave me his answer. "I've never seen them before. Is it a different language?"

"I don't know. It could be in code." I considered my options. "I could cast a spell to reveal any hidden words, but that could cause damage to the book. I don't want to take that chance."

"I don't want you to either."

"I could take the book to Blythe and see if she can decipher it. She might even recognise this language."

Trent nodded. "But what if Grandma comes back and finds out we've taken it?" He fell silent and stared at the book. His voice was full of fear as he said, "She's not coming back, is she? She'd never leave her book. Something awful has happened to her, hasn't it?"

I replied, "We don't know yet, and we don't know why she left without taking her book."

"But it can't be good, can it? Why would she leave without taking her special book? Unless someone forced her to." His eyes brimmed with tears.

Stanley moved over to Trent and said gently, "We don't know what's happened to her yet. Try to stay strong."

Trent gave Stanley a wobbly smile. "I'll try to." Then he roughly wiped his tears away. He addressed me, "What are we going to do now? Can you get Blythe to look at the book straight away? There could be a clue inside. That's possible, isn't it?"

"It is. I'll take it over to her soon. I'll keep this book safe." I sent a spell over the book to shrink it. I put it in my pocket and then placed a sealing spell on my pocket. I didn't want the book to accidentally fall out. "Where did your grandma spend most of her time? Didn't you mention an area in the forest?"

"Yes, she went there every day to talk about herself. But what's that got to do with anything?"

"Someone in the forest might know something important." I didn't expand on that. I wanted to find out more about Brigid, including any enemies she had. Or has, I corrected myself, hoping she was still alive.

Trent nodded. "Okay. Do you want to go there now?"

"Yes, please."

He spun around and hurried out of the door. Stanley and I went after him. I called out, "Slow down!"

He did slow down, but not by much. Not happy with having to run behind him, I sneakily cast a slowing-down spell on him. He was oblivious to it and carried on walking but at a better pace for Stanley and me.

Stanley padded at my side and as we entered The Forest Zone, he said, "I love these blue flowers. They're everywhere." He looked upwards. "And I love all the walkways between the trees. I'd love to explore them."

I followed his gaze. "I would too, if we had the time. I like the tree houses. They look so cute. I bet they're all cozy inside."

"Cozy with a great view."

We were too busy looking up that we didn't watch where we were going. We bumped into Trent who had come to a sudden stop in front of us.

He didn't even register us. He was trembling with rage at something ahead of us. He seethed, "What's he doing here?"

Chapter 8

Trent dashed forward, but thanks to my spell, he didn't move as quickly as he expected to. I grabbed his arm and restrained him.

"Let me go!" he demanded.

"No. If you're going to be a witch, you really have to control your impetuous side," I told him. "Tell me who's annoyed you now."

"It's him." Trent nodded his head in the direction of a cloaked figure who was sitting in a large, carved wooden chair. The chair was in front of a tree which had glittering lights floating around its bark. An audience was seated on the ground in front of the cloaked figure, listening to what he was saying. Trent snapped, "How dare he sit in Grandma's chair!"

"Who is it?"

Stanley said to me, "I think it's one of those wizards. He looks like his statue."

I released Trent with a stern stare, and then took my phone out and had a quick look at the photos I'd taken. "Oh, yes. It's the first wizard in the line. Trent, what's his name?"

"Arestrum," Trent said with a snarl. He rolled his jumper sleeves up. They immediately fell back down his thin arms. "I'm going to give him a piece of my mind."

"No, you're not. Stay right where you are. I want to hear what he's saying."

Trent grumbled and muttered to himself. I picked Stanley up so he could see Arestrum better. The wizard's loud voice came to us clearly.

"So there I was," Arestrum told his rapt audience. "In the middle of three enormous dragons, all out for my blood. Fire burst from them, licking the edge of my cloak and setting it alight." The audience gasped. "But I stood my ground. One by one, those vicious creatures tried to attack me. But they were no match for me, not with my powerful skills." He paused for dramatic effect.

Someone shouted, "What did you do?"

Arestrum leaned forward, his eyes shining with glee. "I used my cunning and wits against those wicked monsters. I cut them down right where they stood! With a wave of my hand and the right spell, I ended the lives of those fiery fiends!" He sat back in his chair and made a steeple of his fingers. "But those monsters are just the beginning. There are more dragons for me to slay, and that's what I'll do. I'm the only one who's powerful enough to do it. Evil dragons are no match for me. I won't rest until every single one of them has gone."

His audience whooped and clapped.

Stanley said, "I don't understand why he's saying that about dragons. We've met a few, haven't we Cassia? And they were lovely. Not evil at all."

Trent gave Stanley an interested look. "You've met dragons? Really?"

"Yes," Stanley said with a smile. "I can tell you all about them if you like? And some of the other creatures we've met."

Trent's smile was barely perceptible. "I would like that. Thanks."

I shared a quick smile with Stanley before turning my attention back to the gloating wizard.

Arestrum was holding his hands up, waiting for his audience to stop clapping. Once they had, he said, "Do you want to know what I did with those dead dragons?"

"No, I don't," Stanley said in disgust. He put his paws over his ears and said to Trent, "Don't you listen either. It'll only upset you."

Trent hesitated a second before copying Stanley.

I tilted my head. Where was this tale going? Nowhere good by the sound of it.

Arestrum rubbed his hands together gleefully. "I chopped their heads off! And then I boiled their bones!"

There was a stunned silence.

But not from me. Anger burst through me. Despite telling Trent a witch needed to restrain themselves, I swiftly passed Stanley to Trent and then strode towards Arestrum.

Creatures sitting on the ground turned as they watched me march towards the wizard.

I came to a stop in front of him and asked angrily, "You did what to those dragons?"

He was too stunned to speak for a moment. But he soon found his voice. "I chopped their heads off and boiled their bones. And that's what they deserved."

"Really? What did they do which was so bad? Hmm?" I could barely control my anger. "I'm waiting."

Arestrum glanced away from me. "It's none of your business."

"I'm making it my business. You can't go around killing dragons and then mutilating them. I demand to know what they did." I looked over my shoulder. "I'm sure everyone else wants to know too. Unless you've already told them before I got here?"

Someone piped up, "We don't know what the dragons did. He missed that part out."

I turned back to Arestrum. "Well? We all want to know."

Quick as a flash, the wizard leapt to his feet and aimed a spell at me. I ducked to the side, but the spell caught my hair and I could smell it burning. One wave of my hand put the fire out.

I was furious now. "How dare you cast a spell like that! You could have hurt anyone in the audience!"

The wizard smirked and raised his hand at me. "I can do what I like. I'm Arestrum The Great!"

I heard Trent shout, "No you're not! There's nothing great about you."

Arestrum had a sneaky look in his eyes as if planning his next attack on me. I didn't give him the time to do any further damage. I sent a magical rope around his body, making sure his arms were pulled to his sides.

"How dare you!" Arestrum struggled against the rope. "Release me immediately! I command it."

I turned my back on him and addressed the seated residents. "I think it's best if you leave. I need to have a talk with Arestrum. I can't take the chance of him using more magic and hurting one of you."

Arestrum yelled, "Don't listen to her! She's a nobody!"

A wrinkly vampire stood up with a bit of difficulty. He said, "She's not a nobody. She's Cassia Winter. A justice witch from Brimstone." He smiled at me showing very white fangs. "I know your gran, Cassia. How is she?"

"She's fine, thank you."

"And what about Blythe? I've been wanting to pay her a visit, but you know how time runs away with you."

Chuckles came from the audience. More of them were standing now. A worrying amount of creaks accompanied their standing up movements along with many groans.

I said to the vampire, "Blythe is great. I'd better get back to Arestrum." I half turned.

The vampire hadn't finished with me yet. "How's that young fella of yours? Luca, isn't it? You've been together a while now haven't you? Any signs of a marriage? I love a good wedding."

My cheeks warmed up. I didn't want to discuss my private life right now, and not in front of so many creatures who now looked at me with interest. I replied, "Luca is well. I really must get back to my work." I jerked my thumb at the restrained wizard.

"Of course, of course. Don't let us keep you. Give my love to your gran and Blythe." He gave me a wave before walking away. The other creatures went with him.

As the area in front of us cleared, I noticed Trent was half-hidden behind a tree. Stanley was still in his arms.

Trent said, "Is it safe to come out now? I didn't want Stanley to get hurt with all that magic being thrown around."

His concern about Stanley made me smile. I said, "It's safe now. Come over here, but stay back a bit." My smile dropped as I turned to face the wizard.

Fire blazed in his eyes. "So, you're a justice witch then. Are you here about those witches?" His lips pulled back in a snarl. "I'm glad they've gone. And I'm glad they're never coming back."

I took two steps forward and looked him straight in the eyes. "How do you know they're never coming back?"

Chapter 9

Arestrum looked flustered. "Well, I just assumed. The witches vanished so suddenly and without explanation. I presumed they'd left forever." His glance darted left and right as if looking for an escape route.

Trent cried out, "You liar! You did something to them!" His loud words startled Stanley and Trent was instantly contrite. "Sorry, I didn't mean to scare you." He gently placed Stanley on the ground and continued berating the captive wizard. "You moved Grandma's statue! You put yours in her place!"

I winced. "Trent, stop shouting."

"You shouted at him. Why can't I?"

"I'm not going to shout at him again, and neither are you. Okay?"

"Okay," he replied in a sulky tone.

I gave Arestrum my full attention. "Did you move those stone figures?"

He lifted his chin. "I'm not saying another word until you release me from this rope."

"Fair enough," I said. "I'll transport you back to Brimstone, put you in a cell and release the rope there. Then we can talk."

"You can't do that!" There was a hint of worry in his voice.

"I can, and I will. Unless you talk now."

Arestrum looked as if he were having a battle with his thoughts. "Okay," he relented. "I'll talk. What do you want to know?"

Trent opened his mouth, but I put my hand up to silence him. I said, "Let's start with those statues by the clubhouse. Did you move them?"

"No. I thought Brigid had. She was the one who put them there in the first place. I presumed she moved them too."

"Why would she do that?" I asked.

"I don't know. Perhaps she knew she'd been leaving soon and she wanted someone powerful to take the head of the line."

Trent made a snorting noise.

I continued with my questions. "What do you know about her disappearance?"

He looked as if he were trying to shrug, but the magical rope wouldn't allow it. "I don't know. One day she was here, and the next she wasn't. I did think it was strange she'd leave without telling anyone. And it's weird that the other witches went with her. I just assumed they had urgent business to attend to." He shot a look at Trent. "Didn't your grandma always say that witches never retire?"

Trent mumbled begrudgingly, "She might have."

Arestrum nodded. "So, I thought she'd left the village on witch business."

"Okay." I gave him a closer look. Was he telling me the truth?

The wizard said, "When did you last check the figures?"

"Not that long ago," I said. "Why?"

"You do know about the shrinkage, don't you?"

"No. What do you mean?"

Arestrum sent a swift look at Trent before looking at me. "The statues disappear when someone dies. It was Brigid's idea for that to happen. If a resident is seriously ill and death is imminent, their statue will start to shrink." A flash of sadness crossed his face. "The figure of Brigid has shrunk. I noticed it a few hours ago. The other witches have got smaller too."

Trent stiffened. "What? Are you sure?"

Arestrum nodded.

"But..." Trent shook his head as if trying to make sense of the wizard's words. "What does that mean?"

Arestrum's tone was surprisingly soft as he replied, "Your Grandma could be dying. Or, at least, be in danger."

"No! You're lying!" Trent grabbed my arm. "We have to get back to the statues! I have to look at them right now! Come on."

I was eager to look at them too, but I had more questions for the wizard. I said to Trent, "You go. And then come straight back here." I released the slowing-down spell discreetly from him.

Trent gulped. "Okay. Yes. I'll do that. But what if...?"

Stanley said, "I'll come with you, Trent. If you like?"

Trent gave Stanley a thankful smile. "Yes, I would like that. Thanks."

Stanley sent me a swift smile before leaving the area with Trent.

I said to Arestrum, "It's just us now. Tell me everything you know about the witches."

He sighed. "Can't you release me from this rope? It's cutting into my elbows."

"No. Not yet."

"Okay. I suppose I'd do the same in your shoes. I'll tell you about the witches. I'll start with the quiet one. What's her name? I always forget it."

"Edie?"

"That's her." He frowned. "I'll be honest, I don't know much about her. I must have spoken to her at some point. She's very forgettable. I know about the other one, Avalon. She's not the least bit forgettable. So loud and full of herself. Thinks everyone is in love with her. She toys with hearts just for the fun of it." His voice turned bitter.

"Did she toy with your heart?"

"What? Of course not! We barely spoke to each other. She spends most of her time at The Fun Zone. I never go there, ever. But that doesn't stop me from hearing what Avalon gets up to whilst she's there. And every evening when she comes home, she sings and dances all the way through the village. She doesn't give a hoot who she wakes up."

I recalled Trent's comments about Brigid and Avalon. "Did Brigid know about her behaviour?"

"Of course. We all did. I complained to Brigid many times and told her to do something."

"And did she?"

"Not that I know off." He pressed his lips together and gave me a long look. "Between you and me, I admired Brigid. But if you ever tell anyone that, I'll deny it."

"Why did you admire her?"

He smiled. "She had done so much in her time. She'd had so many adventures. And she knew many, many spells. She was a wonderful storyteller. I used to hide behind that tree over there and listen to her. She held her audience's attention from the second she began speaking. She was amazing."

I nodded. "You keep talking about her in the past tense."

"Do I?" His head dropped. "I suppose I'm fearing the worst. I know how much Brigid loves that skinny grandson of hers. She wouldn't leave without telling him, which makes me think someone forced her to leave. Something is wrong. I can feel it."

"Did Brigid have any enemies?"

"Just me," he said with a small smile. "But it was all show. I had a lot of respect for her, but I didn't want her to know that. When I came here a few weeks ago to listen to her tales, I was surprised and disappointed when she didn't turn up. I came back every day, hoping she'd return. But she didn't. I asked around, but no one knew where she'd gone. I think we all assumed she had left on a witch-related issue."

"Why have you taken up her place here?"

"Someone had to. I've been listening to Brigid's tales for a long time, and I knew most of them by heart. So, I decided to entertain her audience until she returned. I used her stories and turned them around a bit." He shook his head slowly. "It's hard work coming up with so many stories. I do hope she comes back soon. I miss her."

I couldn't decide if he was lying or not. I asked, "That tale about the dragons, was it true? Did you base it on one of Brigid's stories? Did Brigid actually kill dragons?"

"No, she didn't. And neither did I. I don't know why I came up with that story. I knew I'd gone too far as soon as the words came out of my mouth. I apologise. I should never have started regurgitating Brigid's tales in the first place."

Someone came crashing through the bushes. It was Stanley.

He stopped at my side and panted. "Come quickly! It's Trent!"

Chapter 10

"Trent? What's happened to him?" I asked.

"He's in trouble. Follow me." Stanley spun around and began to run back along the path.

"Stanley! Stop right there. I'm not doing any more running today, not when I've got my broomstick here."

Stanley swivelled on the spot and came back to me. "Excellent idea. My paws are getting very sore."

We got on my broomstick. I looked over at Arestrum, released him from the magical rope and said, "I haven't finished talking to you yet. I'll come back later."

"I'm sure you will," Arestrum said with a sigh. He sank into the chair. "I'll wait for you here."

As soon as we were airborne, I said to Stanley, "Where is Trent? Why is he in trouble? And have the statues changed at all?"

"The statues look just the same. But while we were looking at them, Trent got it into his head that he should ask residents about Avalon because that would lead to his grandma. He headed off to The Fun Zone, and that's when he got into trouble."

I turned my broomstick in the direction of The Fun Zone. It soon came into view. "What sort of trouble?"

Stanley aimed his paw downwards. "You can see for yourself. There he is. I think that creature holding him captive is a satyr. He's got goat legs, a human top bit and horns. That is a satyr, isn't it?"

I looked closer. "It is."

We headed to the ground and stopped next to the satyr who suddenly looked too big. He was wearing a shirt which had the name of the retirement village on it. Those Mirella Phlox flowers had been embroidered under the words. The shirt looked too small on the muscular creature as if it could rip at any moment. His denim shorts were having the same struggle as they tried valiantly to cover the satyr's hairy legs.

Trent had been bound head to toe in a thick rope. His face was white and there was terror in his eyes. He couldn't speak because a piece of blue cloth was around his mouth.

What had Trent done to deserve such harsh treatment?

I stepped closer to him. The satyr immediately blocked me and snapped, "Back away from the prisoner!"

"Prisoner? What has he done?" I asked.

"He tried to enter The Fun Zone without a resident with him."

"Is that all?"

The satyr's chest inflated. "Is that all? Is that all?" His nostrils flared. "I don't know where you come from, but we have strict rules and regulations here. Our residents are our top priority. We can't have," he paused and disgust filled his face, "non-residents thinking they can go wherever they want to. This place would fall apart if we allowed that."

A whimper came from Trent. His face was almost chalk-white now.

I said to the satyr, "Release him. He looks in pain."

"You can't tell me what to do. You're a non-resident too. You shouldn't be here either. Clear off before I tie you up too. And your cat."

I stood as tall as I could. "I have permission to be here."

"Oh yeah? Who from?"

"From Blythe. In Brimstone."

The satyr stared at me and didn't say a word.

I continued, "We're looking into the disappearance of Brigid, Edie and Avalon."

"Avalon?" The satyr's huge shoulders sagged. "She's missing? I thought she'd just gone on holiday. What's happened to her? Has someone taken her? Has someone hurt that beautiful witch?"

"We don't know what's happened to her yet." I nodded in Trent's direction. "Trent here is helping with our investigation."

The satyr turned to Trent and released him in a flash. He grabbed Trent by the shoulder. "Why didn't you tell me about Avalon?"

Trent rubbed his wrists. "You never gave me the chance." With some effort, he freed himself from the satyr's big hand. "Can we go into The Fun Zone now?"

"Yes! Go! Find that wonderful witch! Do you need my help?"

Trent raised his eyebrows in my direction.

I said to the satyr, "No. Thank you." It was obvious the satyr liked Avalon, and I wondered whether I should ask my next question or not. I decided to ask him. "Are you one of Avalon's ex-husbands?"

The satyr sighed. "I should be so lucky." He sighed again and a dreamy look came into his eyes. "I do think about it. A lot. A satyr can dream can't he?"

Stanley said, "Anyone can dream. And dreams do come true sometimes."

The satyr smiled down at Stanley. He moved to one side to allow us to enter The Fun Zone. "Please, find her."

"We'll do our best," Stanley said.

I didn't speak to Trent until we were away from the satyr. Then I let him have it. "What did you think you were doing? I told you I was in charge of this investigation. You were supposed to look at the stone figures and then come back to me."

He didn't look at me. "But you're taking too long about everything. I had to do something. I have to find Grandma. She needs me." His voice broke on the last word.

"Just don't go rushing off on your own again. Okay?"

He nodded. "Okay."

We walked along a light-coloured path which took us to the first of many roller coasters. The carriages on the roller coaster were in the shape of dragons.

Stanley cried out, "Trent! Look! Dragon carriages."

"Wow!" Trent stared at them. "They look like fun."

Stanley cast me a hopeful look. I knew what he was thinking. I said gently, "No. We don't have time for fun. We've got work to do."

"Of course," Stanley said. His attention was drawn to something else. "Trent! Look! Flying carpets. You can fly them yourself!"

Trent's mouth fell open. "I would love to go on them. Look how high they go."

"I know! They fly all over this area."

Stanley and Trent watched in amazement as a brightly coloured rug flew over our heads. It was being flown by a laughing goblin who looked as if he were having the time of his life.

Stanley's voice was full of awe. "I love this place. Cassia, when can I retire? Am I old enough yet?"

"I want to retire too," Trent added. "Then I would come here every day."

"You're both too young to retire. Walk on," I told the pair.

I heard a tut coming from one of them, but I ignored it.

We didn't get far before Stanley yelled, "Racing unicorns! Look at them go!"

Trent swooped Stanley up. "Look over there! There's an exploding volcano and people are riding down the side of it. I wish we could go on that."

"Me too," Stanley added wistfully.

They both looked my way. I felt like a mother in charge of excited toddlers. "We've got work to do," I repeated firmly.

Trent said, "You might get on better if I wasn't in your way. You keep saying I'm getting in your way."

"I don't think I did."

Trent continued, "And you know how quickly I get annoyed at how slowly things are going. I should give you some space."

"And you keep running away," Stanley put in. "And Cassia has to keep running after you."

"That's true. I do keep doing that." Trent looked as if he'd suddenly thought of the perfect solution. "But if I go on some of the rides here, then Cassia would know exactly where I am."

"That sounds like an excellent idea," Stanley said with a nod. "And I should stay with you. To keep an eye on you."

Once again, they gave me beseeching looks.

I knew when I was beaten. I said, "Trent, have you been in this area before?"

"No. Grandma wouldn't let me. I think it's because of the nightclubs and the residents who go there. Grandma said certain residents couldn't be trusted once they'd been in a nightclub for a few hours."

"Avalon spent a lot of time in the nightclubs," I recalled. "So, I need to visit them and start asking questions about her." I smiled at them. "I can do that on my own. You two stay in this area."

"Oh, we can't leave you to do the work on your own," Stanley said unconvincingly.

I stroked his little head. "You can. I'll be fine. You have some fun with Trent."

Stanley grinned. "Thank you. I love you."

"Love you too." I wagged my finger at him. "Don't do anything dangerous."

"We won't," he assured me. He looked at Trent. "Flying carpets first?"

"Yes!" Trent turned away with Stanley firmly tucked in his arms.

As they walked away, I heard Stanley say, "I'll fly the carpet first. Then you can have a go. I'm not scared of flying. I've flown Cassia's broomstick on my own."

"Have you? I didn't know cats could do that. Wow."

They walked away chatting about which rides they should go on after the flying carpets. I was glad Trent was out of the way because it would allow me to talk more freely to residents about his grandma. And I would rather go into the nightclubs on my own.

I saw signs for the nightclubs and headed that way. As I did so, the hairs on the back of my neck began to lift.

Someone was following me.

Chapter 11

I looked behind me but didn't see anyone there. Yet the feeling of being followed persisted.

Setting off at a slow walk, and still aware of someone watching me, I took in the sights on either side of me. The rides became larger and noisier for a while, but as I walked along they became sparser. Smells of cooked food wafted up my nose. If I hadn't been so aware of my unknown companion, I would have been tempted to buy something from the many vendors along the street.

The sight of the Mirella Phlox dotted everywhere did lift my spirits a tad.

Whilst the residents around me appeared to be in their later years, the smiles on their faces and the joy in their cries made them seem much younger. No wonder Blythe said she wouldn't be able to leave if she came here. It really was a lovely place.

Apart from the missing witches, devious wizards and the increasing feeling of doom which was running through me.

My steps increased in pace. The rides were now replaced by wooden huts selling a variety of potions which I didn't recognise. Queues formed in front of the huts. When the residents caught me looking their way, they quickly avoided my gaze. They most definitely looked shifty. What was being sold in those huts?

I came to a line of single-storey buildings. Names above their doors lit up in neon-like lights. I stopped at the first one which was called The Howling Werewolf. I took my phone out and clicked on the mirror facility. I held it to the left of my face so I could see if anyone was following me.

There was no one there.

I put the phone away and mentally reminded myself to ask Blythe if there were any spells which would put eyes in the back of my head. Only temporarily, of course.

I couldn't shake the feeling of unease as I went through the nightclub doors and down some steps. I walked along a short hallway and through a double set of gold, sparkly doors.

Through the doors was a dimly lit room. It took a moment for my eyes to adjust to the darkness. When I did, I saw a round dance floor with tables surrounding it. A few of the tables were occupied by solitary figures holding glasses of whatever liquid they were having. None of them looked my way.

I quickly crossed the dance floor until I reached the bar. I rested my hands on the bar and cast a fearful glance at the double doors behind me. Was someone still following me? I brought to mind all the defensive spells which I knew in case I would need them.

"Hello there!" A satyr suddenly popped up from behind the bar causing me to shriek in surprise.

I put my hand over my chest in an effort to still my thudding heart. "Where did you come from?"

"Sorry about that, gorgeous. I didn't mean to scare you." The satyr gave me a broad grin. Even though there wasn't much light in the nightclub, I could see the glint of mischief in his eyes. "What can I do for you? Your wish is my command. Do what you want with me." He held his arms out wide.

Heat flooded my face as I took in his appearance. Here was yet another satyr with more than his fair share of muscles. But this one was bare-chested which didn't leave much to the imagination. And I had a vivid imagination. He was wearing very tight gold shorts which were in danger of cutting off his circulation. The mischievous glint in his brown eyes intensified as he caught me looking him over, which I was trying not to do.

I cleared my throat and said, "Hello. I'm sorry to disturb you."

"You're not disturbing me at all, beautiful. What a treat for me to have such a vision of loveliness walk in here. Be still my beating heart." He placed his hand over his thick chest. "Here on your own, are you? Want some company?" His muscles actually flexed as he spoke.

I placed my attention firmly on his face. "I don't need any company, thank you. But I'd like to ask you some questions."

"And I will answer every one of them. But first, let me get you a drink. On the house." His hand moved from his chest to the row of bottles behind him. "Anything you want. Anything."

"No, thank you." My voice was prim, but my eyes were struggling to stay on his face and not his chest. What was going on here? Was there magic in the air? "I'm Cassia Winter. I'm a justice witch from Brimstone. I'm looking into the disappearance of some residents."

"Cassia." He smiled. "What a beautiful name. So poetic. And a witch too? Of course you are. You bewitched me from the second I saw you." He reached out a hand and placed it on my arm. It was surprisingly hot. "And here on business. Difficult business by the hint of worry in your alluring eyes."

I blinked. I was quite sure my eyes were not alluring. I pulled my arm free. "I understand another witch, Avalon, used to visit nightclubs here. Do you know her? Did she ever come here?"

He nodded. "Yes, she came here often. Life and soul of the party when she's here. Beautiful, and she knows it. Not like you, Cassia. I imagine you don't know how beautiful you are." He heaved a heavy sigh which hit me in the face. His breath was incredibly hot and I couldn't help wincing.

"When did you last see her?"

He shrugged. "A few weeks ago, I think. You have amazing eyes, my Cassia. I'd better not gaze upon you too much for I fear I will fall madly in love with you." He held his hands up. "Oops. Too late. I have fallen. I need to know everything about you, my love."

"I'm not here to talk about myself," I said as confidentially as I could. His direct look was making me feel hot and embarrassed. I suddenly wished Stanley was here with me. "Did Avalon have any enemies?"

"Plenty. Lots of creatures were jealous of her looks and ways. And it wasn't just in the nightclubs. Whenever I saw her around the village with those witch friends of hers, I got the feeling they didn't like her much. But she had many male admirers. Not me, though. I prefer a gentler beauty. Like you. Let's put some music on and have a dance." He held his hand out.

I ignored it. "I understand Avalon was married fifteen times, and that some of her ex-husbands live around here. Do you know who they are?"

He withdrew his hand. "I do. One of them has been bothering her a lot recently. He comes here all the time and pesters her. He couldn't accept their marriage was over. I had to throw him out a few times. Do you believe in love at first sight, my wonderful witch?"

"No. Who was this resident?"

"He's called Meevan." He frowned. "I think he's added an extra bit to his name recently. He goes by the name of Meevan The Marvellous. Although, I don't know what's so marvellous about him. More like Meevan The Miserable."

My heart quickened. "Is he a wizard?"

"He is." His gaze lingered on my face. "How intelligent you are. Tell me, can you read minds? Do you know what I'm thinking right now?"

I could guess, but I refused to let my mind go there. I took my phone out, tapped on the photo of the stone wizards and held it up. "Is Meevan one of these?"

The satyr took a sharp intake of breath. "What amazing magic is this? You must have so much talent to produce such an enchanted item." He swiftly put his hot hand around mine and pulled the phone closer taking me with it. "Yes, that's him in the middle."

I pulled my hand and phone free. "Where will I find him?"

In a flash, he leapt over the bar and said, "I will take you to him. I can't bear the thought of us being apart even for a second."

"I can manage on my own, thank you."

He dramatically fell to his knees. "No! You mustn't leave me, Cassia Winter. My heart will break." He rested his head against my legs.

I took two steps back until his head was no longer touching me. "I'll find him on my own." I made to turn away.

The satyr jumped to his feet. "I must come with you. I can't let you walk around this village on your own."

"You can. Goodbye." I began to walk away.

"Wait!" he called out. "If you insist on leaving me so abruptly, let us have one last kiss goodbye."

I carried on walking. "We haven't even had a first kiss. And we're not going to. Goodbye."

"Noooo! Don't leave me!" he wailed.

I broke into a jog. A hooded creature at a table muttered, "The wizard is in the nightclub next door. Run away before that seducing satyr convinces you to stay."

"Thanks," I replied before racing towards the doors and through them. Up the steps I went at a speed which I'd never used before. I didn't even stop when I got out of the nightclub. I turned swiftly to the right and dashed into the next building.

Once down the steps and through the double doors, I came to a sudden stop. There was someone right behind me.

Chapter 12

I turned around, but there was no one there. But someone had been behind me; I had sensed it.

A sudden feeling of despair came over me causing me to fall against the wall. My knees buckled and I slid to the floor, my heart pounding. I took some deep breaths and blew them out slowly. The despair left me. I shakily got to my feet.

What had just happened? Had someone cast a spell on me? If so, why? To stop me making more enquiries?

Well, that wasn't going to happen. With grim determination, I walked through a pair of silver doors and into a room which looked similar to the nightclub I'd just left. It wasn't as dark in here and I could see the occupants clearly. There were more of them in here, but they were all sitting at the same angle with their backs facing the dance floor.

My ears soon told me why that was.

An awful dull droning sound was coming from someone in the middle of the dance floor. I looked that way to see a figure sitting on a stool and crooning into a microphone. He was clad in black clothes which had silver threads running through them. A black cloak hung around his shoulders, again with silver running through it. His dark hair matched his outfit, the silver in his hair catching the overhead lights.

I winced. The noise coming from him was truly terrible. A quick glance at my phone showed him to be Meevan. What had the satyr called him? Meevan The Marvellous? He didn't look marvellous. He looked dejected and full of doom and gloom. I paid attention to the words he was singing.

"I am an empty vessel," he moaned. "My heart is in one thousand pieces since you left."

I frowned. If he was an empty vessel, would bits of his heart still be in his body?

He continued to wail. "My nights are restless as I wander the streets looking for you. Sleep is no longer my friend." He shook his head sorrowfully. "My dreams are full of your face. My ears overflowing with your laughter."

My eyes narrowed. His song wasn't making any sense at all. And it was making my ears hurt. I had to interrupt him.

His voice suddenly rose. "My eyes ache with pain because I will never see your sweet face again! My lips will never kiss your soft lips again!"

Someone seated at a table yelled, "Give it a rest! You're giving me a headache."

Someone else added, "You're giving me a headache, a stomach ache and earache with your miserable words. I came in for a quiet drink, not to be tortured. Clear off and take your misery with you!"

Meevan glared at the speaker, shifted on his stool a little and looked as if he were going to start singing again.

I rushed forward before he could do so. "Hello! Sorry to disturb you. Can I ask you some questions about Avalon, please?"

Meevan dropped his microphone, jumped to his feet and grabbed my shoulders. "Avalon! Have you found her? Have you brought my true love back to me? Where is she? I need to see her immediately."

I freed myself from his grip. "I haven't found her. Sorry."

He let out a piercing wail. "My heart!" He clutched his chest and fell to the floor.

"Is he dead?" a voice called out. "Thank the goblins for that. We can have some peace now."

I hoped he wasn't dead. I crouched at Meevan's side and gave him a gentle shake. I heard quiet sobs coming from him. Phew. He was still alive.

I asked him, "Are you okay? Can you talk? I'm looking for Avalon, and I could do with your help. Can you talk to me about her?"

He pulled himself into a sitting position and wiped tears from his cheeks. He gave me a suspicious look. "Who are you? And why are you asking questions about my beloved wife?"

"Wife? I thought you weren't married anymore." I sat next to him.

His head dropped at my words. "Separating was a big mistake. Avalon knows that. We'll soon be back together. I know we will." He lifted his head. "Tell me who you are."

I gave him that information and added, "I'm looking for Avalon, and the other witches too. What can you tell me about her friends, Brigid and Edie?"

He waved his hand dismissively. "Friends! Ha! I wouldn't call them that. They poisoned Avalon's mind against me. They saw how happy we were together, and that made them jealous. They made Avalon fall out of love with me. No doubt using black magic." His eyes narrowed. "Brigid is too full of herself. She wants to be in charge of everyone. She hates Avalon having fun, she said it's not right for witches to have so much fun. And that other one, what's her name again?"

"Edie."

"Yes. Edie. She was always whispering to Avalon about something or other. Whispering spells into her ears, I suspect. But it's Brigid who's the evil one. She made Avalon turn cold on me. To reject my love." His hands were curled into fists.

I said carefully, "When did you separate?"

"About six months ago." His fists unclenched. "My life hasn't been the same since. I've been in a dark pit of misery since she went missing."

"How do you know she's gone missing? She could have gone on holiday or left for business reasons."

He gave me a small smile. "She wouldn't do that without telling me. Even though we're not legally together, our hearts are still connected. She would have said something to me if she were going on holiday. She wouldn't want me to worry. No, something has happened to her. Someone has stolen my beautiful wife away."

I didn't want to correct him over the wife comment again. I asked, "When did you notice she was missing?"

"Two weeks ago. I check on her every day. It's not spying or anything weird. I merely wait by her home until she gets up. Then I accompany her throughout the day, at a distance, of course. And I turn up to the nightclubs she visits and sing her one of my beautiful songs. She pretends to be angry with me, but I know that's because of the spell Brigid and the other one have cast on her."

I didn't comment on his stalking. As she's a witch, I'm sure Avalon would have been fully aware that Meevan was following her all the time. Was that why she left the village?

Knowing I was going to upset him, but doing so anyway, I asked, "What do you know about her other husbands? Is she married to someone else now?"

A mask of rage descended over Meevan's face changing his features completely. He hissed, "How dare you ask me such a thing! Avalon loves me. Me!"

His anger didn't put me off. I was about to ask more questions about Avalon's marriages but a figure came racing towards us.

"Cassia! Cassia!" It was Trent. He dashed to my side and fell to his knees. His face was ashen, and his whole body was trembling. His breaths were laboured as he struggled to speak.

I put my hand on his arm. "Calm down. Take a deep breath. Tell me what's wrong. Take your time."

Tears spilled from his eyes. "Cassia. It's Stanley."

"What about him?"

He gulped. "He's dead. Cassia, Stanley is dead."

Chapter 13

I stared at Trent. "Pardon?"

Trent's mouth opened and closed, but I couldn't hear his words. There was a dull buzzing sound in my ears.

Trent stood up and waved his arms frantically as he continued talking. What was he trying to tell me? Why was he crying?

Trent roughly grabbed my elbow and pulled me from the floor. He shook me and yelled right in my ear. "Cassia! It's Stanley!"

"Pardon? I don't understand."

He dragged me away from the dance floor and up the stairs. He was still talking, but the buzzing in my ears blotted out his words.

As we got to the top of the steps, my knees felt weak and my vision swam. Something terrible had happened. Trent was trying to tell me that, but my brain wouldn't let the words in.

Trent looked at me as we reached the exit doors. "We have to go to him. Right now." He pulled me through the door and into the bright sunlight.

"Who are you talking about?"

"Stanley. I told you." He gave me a searching look. "He's dead."

I yanked my arm free. "No, he isn't."

"He is. There's been an accident."

"Stop lying. That's an awful thing to lie about."

"I'm not lying. Come on! You might be able to do something." For a skinny person, he had a lot of strength in him. He pulled me along the street so quickly that my feet almost left the ground.

As we rushed along, he said, "It was the flying carpets. Stanley flew ours for a bit, then I had a go. Then that other carpet came out of nowhere. I swerved. And Stanley...he fell off."

"What? I don't understand any of this."

We came to a group of residents on the path. They were looking down at something. As if sensing my arrival, they parted and made a path for me.

And there he was.

Stanley.

Lying on the path.

His little grey body.

Not moving.

Not breathing.

I collapsed and let out a noise which I didn't even recognise.

Trent gripped my arm and pulled me up. "There's no time for that! Do something! Bring him back to life. Use your magic!" He shoved me towards the little body.

I dropped to my knees next to the still body. "Stanley? Wake up. Talk to me."

Trent knelt at my side. "He's not asleep. He's dead! Bring him back."

My hands shook as I held them over Stanley's body. I didn't have a spell for bringing the dead back to life. My confused mind tried to recall the spells in Gran's books. I had never seen such a spell. But I had to do something.

I forced as much magic as I could into my hands and kept them over Stanley's unmoving chest. My fingers tingled. I sent more magic to them and over my friend. They prickled. More magic was needed. Soon, my fingers were throbbing in agony and I clenched my teeth to stop myself crying out in pain. I pleaded, "Stanley. Please."

Stanley didn't move. His chest stayed still. His heart didn't beat.

Trent whispered, "It's not working. Why isn't your magic working?"

"I don't know." My eyes filled with useless tears. "I don't know what to do."

I tried again and again, but my magic failed me.

Had Stanley gone forever?

Trent slapped me on the arm. "The flowers! The Mirella Phlox! They can heal."

"I don't think they'll help him." My arms were aching with pain, but I refused to pull my hands away from Stanley.

Trent jumped up. "They might help. I'm going to find some."

I was aware of him leaving. A few seconds later, he was back.

"Here, you do it." He handed me a bunch of the blue flowers.

I had no idea what to do with them. I gently placed them all over Stanley's body. I put extra ones around his heart. All I could do now was send him my love. I closed my eyes and did that.

Trent suddenly slapped me on the back. "Look! Cassia, look at what's happening!"

I opened my eyes just in time to see the blue flowers dissolving into Stanley's body.

There were gasps of amazement from the residents surrounding us. I'd forgotten they were there.

"I'm getting more flowers." Trent rushed away and came back with more. He gave them to me. "You should do it."

The original flowers had been absorbed into Stanley's body by now. I placed the newer flowers over his heart. They immediately melted.

Then we watched.

Trent cried out, "His whiskers! His whiskers moved. I saw them."

Someone called out, "I saw them too. They twitched!"

I stared at Stanley's chest. I stopped breathing as if hoping Stanley would catch my breath.

His chest moved the tiniest amount.

Trent clutched my shoulder. "Cassia! He's breathing!"

I gently placed my hand on Stanley's chest. I could feel something. "Stanley. Please, breathe." The pulsing feeling beneath my hand increased.

His heartbeat?

Was he alive?

I heard a noise. A quiet meow. It came from Stanley.

Trent burst into tears. "He's alive! He's alive!"

Stanley meowed more loudly. His whiskers twitched quickly. He slowly lifted his head and looked my way. He let out a chuckle and said, "What am I doing down here? I'm supposed to be flying a carpet."

The residents around me burst into a mixture of applause and happy cheers.

"Keep still," I told him thickly. "I want to check you for broken bones." I cast the appropriate magic into my hands and hovered them over Stanley's body. I didn't sense any broken parts.

I tenderly lifted my dear friend and pulled him close to me. I could hear his heart beating at full strength now. I muttered, "You're alive. Alive."

Stanley nuzzled his head into my neck. "Was I dead? I don't remember that. Don't cry. You know how blotchy you get when you cry. You're making my fur very soggy."

"I don't care."

I held my dear cat next to me and didn't move for the next few minutes. I heard Trent telling everyone they could leave us now, and that Stanley was fine.

A familiar voice made my eyes snap open. "Is the cat okay?"

It was Arestrum. He had aimed his comments at Trent. What was he doing here? He said he never went to The Fun Zone.

Trent answered him, "Yes, he's fine."

Arestrum sent a quick look my way before saying to Trent, "Weren't you flying the carpet before the cat fell off?"

Colour infused Trent's face. He said, "It was an accident."

"Really?" the wizard asked before quickly walking away, his cloak flapping behind him.

I stared at Trent.

The colour in his face intensified. "Why are you looking at me like that?"

I couldn't answer him.

Had Trent just tried to kill Stanley?

Chapter 14

Trent flung himself to the ground next to Stanley and me. He reached out to Stanley but I swiftly turned so his hand missed. Trent urged, “Stanley, tell Cassia what happened. Tell her how that other flying carpet came out of nowhere. Tell her. Please.”

Stanley got out of my arms and looked at Trent. “I can’t remember much. I know we were flying on our carpet. It was fun. Was I flying it?”

“Yes! And then you told me to have a go. Then that other one shot right at us. You told me to watch out. I swerved, and then you fell off. You must remember.”

“I fell off? Did I?” Stanley looked at me. “Is that why I died? I fell all the way down? Wow. That must have hurt.”

I attempted to pick Stanley up but he moved out of my way and closer to Trent. “I’m sorry, Trent, I can’t remember. You tell Cassia exactly what happened.”

Trent’s head dipped. “She doesn’t believe me. I can tell. She thinks I tried to kill you.” He aimed tear-filled eyes my way. “You do, don’t you?”

I gave him a long look before replying, “It has crossed my mind. But if you did, why would you come and get me? And then get those flowers?”

“Flowers?” Stanley asked. “What flowers? Cassia, you haven’t told me how I came back to life. Did you use a lot of magic on me? I hope you didn’t hurt yourself doing that.”

Trent pulled a bunch of flowers from his pocket. “I thought these might help you. Grandma says they have healing powers. Cassia put these on your body. They melted into you. And then you stopped being dead." He smiled at Stanley. "I'm glad you're not dead anymore."

"Me too." Stanley moved next to Trent and rested his body against Trent's shoulder. "Thank you for bringing me back to life."

"It was Cassia who did it." Trent gently stroked Stanley's head. "I don't know why Grandma doesn't have a cat. I wish I had a friend like you."

"We are friends. Good friends." Stanley gave him a broad smile and then padded over to me. "Trent didn't try to kill me. You know that. Cassia, you have to do one of those memory spells on me. Find out what I saw before I fell off."

I held my hands up. "No! Absolutely not. You're in a delicate state."

"I'm not delicate at all. In fact, I feel better than I have in years." He waved his back leg in the air. "I've had an ache in this leg for months, but it's gone now. I feel years younger."

As if to prove his point, he began to dance up and down the path, wiggling his paws in the air now and again. Trent laughed at his antics. I didn't. I was on edge as if expecting him to collapse at any second.

Once he'd finished his performance, Stanley came over to me and said, "You have to look into my memory." He lowered his voice. "If someone has tried to kill me, they could try again. You don't want that, do you?"

I looked at his little face. He was too clever by half. He knew I wouldn't want him to be in danger.

"Okay," I relented. "But only for a few seconds. Let's move off this path. We're in the way." I picked Stanley up and looked along the path. "Where's my broomstick?"

Trent jumped up. "You left it in the nightclub. I'll get it!" He shot off like a firework.

I took Stanley over to a small grassy area which had clumps of Mirella Phlox dotted around it. Good. I wanted those flowers nearby in case anything should happen to Stanley.

We sat down and I tenderly placed my hands on Stanley's face. His eyes were full of trust which made my eyes prickle with tears. Was I doing the right thing? What if I hurt him?

Stanley said, "You're not going to hurt me if that's what you're thinking. Go on; do your magic." He closed his eyes.

I performed the memory spell on him. The last few minutes of his life came to me in flashes. And then there was blackness. Nothingness. I knew what that meant.

I quickly took my hands off Stanley. He opened his eyes and said, "Well? Did you see anything?"

"Wait for me," Trent called out as he ran over to us holding my broomstick. He put it next to me and sat down cross-legged.

I began, "Stanley, I saw through your eyes. You were on the flying carpet, and you were controlling it. I could feel the adrenaline rushing through you. And you were going far too fast, even though I told you not to."

Stanley let out a guilty chuckle.

I went on. "You told Trent to take the controls. He did. Then a purple carpet came towards you. The front part was tipped up so I couldn't see who was flying it. You saw it and shouted at Trent. You told him to swerve to the left. Then," I paused as I fought to say the words, "there was darkness and I didn't feel anything."

Stanley said matter-of-factly, "That must have been when I died. I'm glad you didn't feel my pain when I landed on the ground, Cassia."

I looked at Trent. "I'm sorry for thinking the worst of you."

"It's okay. I would have thought the same." He looked behind him before continuing, "That wizard, Arestrum, what was he doing here? Do you think he was flying the other carpet?"

"He could have been," I agreed. "And he did try to put the blame on you. I wonder where he is now? I think someone's been following me. It could have been him."

"When was someone following you?" Stanley asked. He looked left and right. "Don't say anything here. Arestrum could be listening to us. Let's leave."

"Excellent idea." I got up and held my arms out towards Stanley.

He said, "Cassia, don't treat me like an invalid. I'm fine. I feel in tip-top condition."

My arms dropped. "Okay. But if you begin to feel weak, you'd better tell me straight away. Let me cast a protection spell on you. At least."

"There's no point," Stanley said. "If that wizard is after us, he'll only remove any protection spells. I think we should head to The Quiet Zone and speak to residents about Edie. And you can tell us about your visits to the nightclubs on the way. Come on you two." He trotted away.

Trent stood up and shared a smile with me. "He's gone very bossy. Why don't you cast the spell anyway? While he's not looking?"

"I already have." My smile increased. "I've put one on you too. If that's okay?"

He blushed and looked at his feet. "It's okay. Thanks. You should put one on yourself as well."

"I will."

Stanley looked over his shoulder. "Hurry up. We haven't got all day."

I picked my broomstick up and went after Stanley. Trent seemed incapable of walking at a normal speed as he jogged ahead of me and caught up with Stanley.

My knees still felt weak as I walked after them. Was Stanley really okay? Or were the flowers only a temporary measure? Would their magic wear off? I wanted to grab Stanley and head back to the safety of Brimstone. But I knew he wouldn't allow that.

I scooped as many blue flowers as I could on my walk along the path. Stanley and Trent were waiting for me just outside the exit of The Fun Zone.

As I reached them, Stanley raised his paw at something behind me. "Look."

I turned around and saw two wizards watching us leave. Arestrum The Great. And Meevan The Marvellous. They both raised their hands in goodbye.

I shivered at the blank expressions on their faces. What were they up to?

Chapter 15

We quickly headed towards The Quiet Zone. My mind didn't feel quiet at all. It was full of suspicious thoughts about those wizards. And I was trying to suppress my fear and worry about Stanley at the same time. I was going to make myself poorly at this rate.

Stanley wasn't helping me feel any better as he talked animatedly about his death. "I've never died before! I can't wait to tell Oliver all about this. Trent, Oliver is my brother. I wonder if he's ever died before?"

Thankfully, Trent said, "Can you stop talking about your death, please? It's making my heart feel very heavy. I can still see you lying on that path."

"Oh. I'm sorry. I won't say another word."

We carried on in silence. After checking there was no one around, I told them about my visits to the nightclubs. I didn't elaborate on the things the flirting satyr in the first club had said to me, but I gave them full details about Meevan.

We had to go by the clubhouse on the way to The Quiet Zone. As we neared the clubhouse, Stanley came to a stop. He said, "Is it just me or have the witch statues got smaller since we last saw them?"

Trent and I stared at the stone figures. I said, "I think they have. I'll take a photo and compare it to the earlier one I took."

Once I had the new photo, I placed it next to the other on my screen and showed them to Trent and Stanley. Going by the trees in the background, it was clear to see that the statues had reduced in size.

After Trent got over the shock of seeing my phone and what it could do, he said, "They are smaller. We're running out of time."

Then, like a wind-up toy, he sped off down the path. To my surprise, Stanley did the same. I didn't. I got on my broomstick and travelled the easy way.

We soon came to The Quiet Zone. There was a satyr standing at the entrance. He was wearing a long robe, and many strands of beads were draped around his neck. He gave us a serene smile and stood to one side, allowing us to enter.

The atmosphere inside immediately calmed me. A little.

The path beneath us was speckled with blue and green stones. Those blue flowers were arranged in neat lines along the path's border. Gentle chanting sounds came from many directions. Even though there was barely a breeze, tall trees swayed from side to side as if dancing. A gentle whispering came from the trees like a soothing serenade.

I could feel some of my worries melting away, but that didn't stop me from keeping most of my attention on Stanley. He turned his head, looked at me and winked.

I asked Trent, "Have you been in this area before?"

"Yeah. Grandma brought me here a few times when she wanted to talk to Edie. Edie runs meditation classes in that area over there. She was popular. I don't know why. It looked boring to me, just sitting there with your eyes closed while Edie talked nonsense. I can't even remember what she said."

"A lot of residents can't remember much about Edie," I said. "That makes me wonder if she had cast a spell on people to make sure that happened."

"Why would she do that?"

"She may have uncovered secrets from residents. Using magic perhaps. And she wouldn't want them to remember that, so she made sure they didn't. Then she might have used that information against them later."

Trent's eyes were wide. "I hadn't thought of that. Do you think she found out an awful secret and tried to blackmail someone? Like a wizard? And the wizard decided to get rid of her. And he got rid of Grandma and Avalon too." He nodded to himself. "That's what's happened. We've worked it out."

"It's only a possibility." I told Trent and Stanley what Arestrum had told me earlier, about him respecting Brigid.

"Rubbish!" Trent declared. "He lied. He lies all the time. He was in The Fun Zone when he said he never went there. He hates Grandma. And that other wizard, Meevan, hates her too. They're behind it. I know they are. Arrest them, Cassia. Arrest them right now." He spun around and made to walk away.

I grabbed his arm. "We haven't got all the facts yet. Come back. Take us to where Edie held her classes. Some of the residents could be waiting for her to return like they did for your grandma."

"It's a waste of time," Trent muttered. He caught my hard glare. "Okay! I'll take you." He stormed off.

"His emotions are tiring me out," I said to Stanley.

Stanley chuckled. "He's young and impetuous."

We followed Trent along the path and around the corner. A chanting noise met us. Along with Trent's raised voice. Now what?

He was standing in front of a creature who was wearing a purple cloak and a silver hat. Lines of sitting creatures were watching Trent as he shouted at the being. Another wizard?

I didn't need to check the photos on my phone to confirm that because Stanley said, "That's the final wizard from the stone figures. Why's Trent shouting at him?"

Trent yelled, "You shouldn't be here! This is Edie's class! What have you done to her? I know you've done something. And your evil wizard friends have done something to my grandma! You're not going to get away with it!"

The wizard placed his hands together and said calmly, "You need to take a deep breath and let your anger go, young witch. After me. Breathe in." He inhaled deeply and closed his eyes.

Trent pushed him over. Gasps came from the seated residents.

"That's enough!" I told Trent as I raced over. I held my hand out to the fallen wizard and helped him up. I looked at Trent and ordered him to apologise.

Trent stuck his chin out defiantly. "No."

The wizard smoothed down his robe and said, "No apology needed. I know he's truly sorry in his heart for attacking me."

"I am not," Trent snapped.

I shot him a warning glance and then addressed the wizard. "We're sorry to disturb you. I'm Cassia Winter, and this is Stanley."

Stanley waved his paw. "Hi! I just died and came back to life. Have you ever done that?"

The wizard stared at Stanley. "Not that I know of."

I now shot a warning glance at Stanley before asking the wizard, "May I take your name, please?"

He bowed his head slightly. "I am Efflon The Wise."

Trent snorted. "The Wise? I don't think so."

Efflon wisely ignored Trent. "I am all knowing and all seeing. Tell me what your business is here."

Trent snorted again. "If you're all knowing and all seeing, then you'd know the answer to that."

I was tempted to put a silencing spell on Trent but restrained myself. "We're looking into the disappearance of Edie and her witch companions. Is this the meditation class which Edie normally takes?"

"It is. I felt it wise to take over when she didn't show up." He gave a benevolent smile to the residents who were still watching us. "Even though I say so myself, I think I'm doing an excellent job."

There was a smattering of feeble applause from the residents.

A resident called out, "Have we finished yet? We've been sitting here for ages. I can't feel my bottom anymore."

Efflon gave the speaker a look which I think was meant to be kind, but it was full of loathing. He said, "You may leave. Our session is over. I wish peace on you all."

There were groans and moans as residents stood up. There were also mumbles of complaints which Efflon ignored.

Once the last resident was out of sight, Efflon whipped his hat off and said, "That Edie has got a lot to answer for! She's let everyone down. If it wasn't for me, there wouldn't be a meditation class here. She's useless, and this village is better off without her." Any peace inside him had apparently vanished.

"Hey!" Trent cried out. "Don't talk about her like that."

"I'll say what I want," Efflon retorted. "That Edie was always sticking her nose in things which didn't concern her. Always creeping up silently, hoping to catch a being in a private conversation. She might have fooled others with her quiet act, but not me. Oh no. Not Efflon The Wise."

"You're not wise at all!" Trent said. "You're nasty and evil, like the other wizards."

A look of pure malice came into Efflon's eyes. "Let me tell you something about your beloved grandma. She was the worst of the witches. Pure evil."

I held my hand up and cast a spell at Trent just before he made a lunge at Efflon. Trent froze in place. I said to the wizard, "Go on. Tell us more about Brigid."

He smiled in a knowing way. "Brigid used black magic. She has done for years. She cast illegal spells. She got rid of anyone who confronted her about it. It's common knowledge here. But everyone's too scared to do anything." His smile grew. "I think someone eventually did find the courage to do something. That's why she's gone."

"Do you know that for certain?"

"No. It's just a feeling."

"If it is a feeling, who do you think would go after her? Arestrum? Meevan?"

He suddenly found his hat very interesting and began to fiddle with the brim, thus avoiding my gaze. "No. They wouldn't do something like that."

"What about you?" I asked. "Did you get rid of them?"

His head snapped up. "Certainly not! How dare you say that? I'm a peaceful creature! I would never hurt another living thing. Never!"

Stanley asked, "Would you hurt a cat? Like me? I died, you know. Someone tried to kill me. But I'm alive again."

Efflon's look was full of confusion. "How did you come back to life? Did your witch use black magic? Only black magic can be used to bring someone back from the dead."

I bristled. "I did not use black magic." I glanced at Stanley. But I would have done in a split second if I'd have known the right spells. I pulled some Mirella Phlox from my pocket. "It was these. They healed Stanley."

"And brought me back from the cold arms of Death," Stanley clarified, rather dramatically.

"Ah, yes." The wizard nodded in a sage manner. "We are lucky to have these marvellous plants around us. They only grow in these parts. I've never seen them anywhere else."

I couldn't look away from the flowers. I had a strong feeling they had something to do with the witches' disappearance. I needed to find out more about them.

Putting the flowers away, I asked Efflon, "Have you got anything to do with the witches going missing?"

"Certainly not! How dare—"

"Do you know for certain who might have hurt them?"

"No! I don't care for the tone in your—"

"Have you been to The Fun Zone in the last thirty minutes?"

Efflon's chest puffed out. "I have not. I wouldn't dirty my boots going in that despicable—"

I cut him off, stared right at him and asked, "Are you keeping anything from me about the witches?"

His face suddenly became blank. His tone was flat as he replied. "No. If there's nothing else, I have things to do." He put his hat back on and walked away.

Stanley shook his head. “He’s a poor liar. Where are we going now? Back to The Fun Zone? We should track Arestrum down and ask him more questions.”

I crouched next to Stanley. “We’re going back to Brimstone. There’s something I have to do.” I stroked his head. “Well, two things actually. And I don’t want any arguments from you.”

Chapter 16

I released Trent from his spell and told him of our intention to return to Brimstone.

"But you haven't found Grandma yet!" he exploded with rage.

I ran my hand over my forehead as if hoping to conjure up some patience.

Stanley came to my rescue. "Trent, Cassia knows what she's doing. She's dealt with many investigations, and she never gives up until she gets to the end of them." He stopped talking, and I knew why. We usually dealt with murders, and I never stopped until I'd found the murderer.

But we weren't dealing with a murder.

Not yet.

Trent gave Stanley a long look. "Are you sure she knows what she's doing?"

"Absolutely." Stanley's voice was full of confidence.

An idea came to me. "Trent, do you want to come with us?"

His mouth fell open. He swallowed and said, "To Brimstone? Really?"

I nodded. "Yep. Have you got a broomstick? You could fit on mine but it'll be a bit of a squash."

"I've got one! I know how to fly it! It's at Grandma's house." He took off like a shot down the path.

Stanley said, "Did you ask him to come with us so he'll stop attacking wizards?"

"Partly," I said with a smile. "And the incident with the flying carpet could have been an attempt on his life and not yours."

"That's a possibility." He bounced from paw to paw energetically. "I'm going to run after him! I'll race him."

I held my hand up. "Whoa! I don't know if I like this new energetic side of you. Running off all the time. Don't expect me to keep up with you. I'm going to fly to Brigid's house. Would you like to join me on the broomstick?" I hesitated. "Or have you become afraid of heights since the, erm, accident?"

"I'm not afraid of anything. Can I fly the broomstick?" He was still hopping from paw to paw.

"No. You're too full of adrenalin." I lowered the broomstick and Stanley hopped on it.

We took off and flew to Brigid's house. Trent came out of the front door as we landed.

He said, "I had a quick look around the house in case Grandma had come home. But she hasn't. Do you think she might have gone to Brimstone? If she was in danger, she might have gone there for help. Might she?" The hope in his eyes was hard to look at.

"Perhaps," was my feeble reply. "Follow us. And I mean follow us. Don't go zooming ahead. Okay?"

"Okay." He sat on his broomstick and leaned forward like a jockey on a racing horse. "I'm ready."

We set off. Trent did race ahead of us a few times, but shouts from me forced him to get behind us. He was hard work. It briefly crossed my mind that Brigid had left the village to have a break from her grandson.

Brimstone came into view. I was overjoyed to see the familiar town. We landed in the middle of the square. Trent's mouth hung open as he took in the surroundings.

I pointed out Blythe's house to him. "I'm going to have a word with Blythe on my own. I'll be over there." I looked down at Stanley. "Will you show Trent around the town? Maybe take him to the café?"

"I will do that," Stanley replied. "And I'll introduce him to some of the residents. Some might know his grandma." He gave me a pointed look. He was going to make discreet enquiries without Trent being aware of it.

Trent pointed to the left. "What's in that shop over there?" His finger moved to another building. "Is that a toy shop? Can we go in there? And where's the café? I'm starving. Come on, Stanley. I want to see everything."

I got down on one knee, cupped Stanley's face in my hand and asked, "How are you feeling?"

"Great. Marvellous. Wonderful. Stop worrying."

"I can't." I released his chin and then watched him walk away with Trent towards the toy shop.

Blythe was waiting for me at the open door of her house. She took one look at my face and said, "Come in. Tell me the bad news. Who's died?"

She put her arm around my shoulders and led me into the living room. She propped my broomstick up, sat me down on the sofa and clicked her fingers. A mug appeared in my hands. Blythe said, "Hot chocolate. With a dash of rum. You need it. Drink."

I took a sip. The thick chocolate slipped down my throat and hit my stomach. A warm feeling soon rushed through my body, no doubt the rum getting to work. I relaxed a little and sat farther back.

She sat opposite me. "Who's dead? One of the witches? All of them?"

I took another drink, needing the calming effects of the rum. My voice was a tad too high as I replied, "No one has died. But those witches are still missing. And I've got at least three suspects; all of them are wizards."

Blythe's mouth curled in disgust. "Wizards. I don't trust them. Flouncing around with their fancy cloaks thinking they're better than anyone else. Start from the beginning. Tell me everything."

I proceeded to tell her almost everything. I couldn't bring myself to talk about Stanley's temporary demise.

Blythe sighed when I'd finished. "You've got your hands full with this one. But you're not on your own. Let me help you with Brigid's book. And let me have a look at those photos you've taken."

I finished the rest of the hot chocolate. The rum had calmed me considerably by now. I took my phone out and handed it to Blythe. She knew how it worked.

She scrolled through the photos. "Ah, yes. I see what you mean. The witch statues do seem smaller in the second photo. That is strange." She continued scrolling through my photos. "Oh, look at these photos of Stanley. He's quite the model, isn't he? So cute."

My eyes stung. I quickly stood up, turned my back on her and removed the sealing spell on my pocket. I took Brigid's tiny book out and made it bigger. I turned around, gave Blythe a bright smile and said, "Here's the book. I can't make any sense of it."

She took the book and began to peruse it. She frowned. "This book has been heavily encrypted. I recognise a few of the symbols, but not many. Brigid has gone to great lengths to disguise what's in here." She looked at me. "But I like a challenge. It might take me a while, but I'll make sense of these scribbles. You mentioned those blue flowers. Have you brought any with you?"

"I have." I pulled a bunch from my pocket. I had a small bouquet in almost every pocket. Just in case. To my surprise, the blue flowers weren't the slightest bit squashed. I gave a few to Blythe.

She rested the flowers in her palm and studied them. "I've never seen these before. They're beautiful. I love the silver and gold flecks in them. Didn't Mrs Tarblast say they have healing powers? I wonder if they have? Or if Mrs Tarblast is having us on."

My eyes began to prickle again. I did my best to fight back my tears. But I lost the battle. I burst into uncontrollable sobs.

Blythe was at my side in a flash. With both her arms around me, she said, "Whatever is the matter? You're keeping something from me. Don't even think of lying to me. I am a wise witch, after all. If you lie to me, I'll be very annoyed. And I'm more than capable of turning you into a cheese sandwich."

Her words caused me to let out an undignified snort. I got control of myself, and through my tears and breaking voice, I told Blythe about Stanley dying.

Her arms dropped from my shoulders. Her face turned white. "Stanley? He died?"

"He's okay now. I think."

"You must take him to Dr Morgan straight away. She'll check him over from nose to tail." Colour came rushing into her cheeks and anger flashed in her eyes. "Who would do that to him? Who?"

"I don't know, but they could have been after Trent," I said.

"That doesn't make it any better." She smoothed my hair from my face. "You must have aged twenty years in the last few hours. I know how close you and Stanley are. I used to have cats when I was younger. I loved them so much, but every time one of them died, a piece of me died with them. It was easier on my heart not to have a cat companion."

"I couldn't do my job without Stanley." I wiped another tear away. Where were they all coming from?

She patted my hand. "I know. You must collect him right now and go to the doctor. Send Trent to me. I'll get some information out of him about his grandma. And I'll make a start on that book of hers. I want this matter sorted out. Whoever hurt Stanley is going to pay the price."

I stood up. "Once Dr Morgan's looked at Stanley, I'll show her these flowers. I'd like to know what they're made of. If they have anything special or unusual in them. I think they have something to do with the witches."

Blythe stood up and gave me a big hug. She said, "We'll get everything settled very soon."

I nodded into her shoulder.

As I left Blythe's house I found Stanley and Trent walking up the path towards me. Trent was eating an ice cream cone which was the size of his head. I told Trent to go into Blythe's house which made his eyes go wide with either fear or delight.

I picked Stanley up and said, "Let's go to the doctor's now. I told you I was going to take you, and I haven't changed my mind."

He chuckled. "I don't know why we have to go. I feel great. There's nothing wrong with me."

I held him closer. I really hoped that was true.

Chapter 17

As always, Dr Morgan was pleased to see us. She was a human but had been living in Brimstone for a long time. She'd attended school with Gran, but looked much younger than my gran. She said it was due to the magical air in Brimstone. I suspected she used the same spells which Blythe used to look young. Despite being human, she knew a handful of spells. Maybe two handfuls.

She gave us a big smile as we entered her office. "I thought I'd be seeing you two soon. I bumped into Mrs Tarblast earlier. She gave me a wink and said to watch out for your return from a certain retirement village. She wouldn't give me any more information than that before she scuttled away. Now then, take a seat and tell me everything."

We sat down in the seats in front of her desk. I kept Stanley on my lap.

Dr Morgan pulled a notepad towards her, picked up a pen and said, "Begin. Has anyone died? Are there any deceased bodies for me to look at?"

My voice was only a little bit wobbly as I said, "We don't have any bodies for you to look at. And that's the problem. Three witches have gone missing from the Mirella Retirement Village. We're at a loss as to where they are."

"I see." She put her pen down. "No bodies? Then why have you come to see me? Unless this is a social visit? Which is lovely as I'm always happy to see you. But from the worry on your face, Cassia, I suspect that isn't the case."

"Could you look at these, please?" I reached into my pocket and pulled some of the blue flowers out. I pushed them across the desk. They still looked fresh as if they'd just been picked. The overhead lights in the office picked up the silver and gold sparkles.

Dr Morgan picked one up. "These are pretty. I haven't seen them before. What are they called?"

"Mirella Phlox."

Her eyebrows rose. "Mirella? The same name as the retirement village?"

I nodded. "Apparently, these flowers only grow in that area. I want to know what these flowers are made of. There's something about them, but I don't know what. I feel they are important for some reason."

Dr Morgan turned the flower over in her hand. "Do you want to know if these have any magic in them? Is that right?"

I nodded and muttered gruffly, "If there is magic in them, I want to know what kind it is. If it's temporary or—" I couldn't get any more words out for the lump in my throat.

Stanley looked at me for a few seconds before turning his head back to the doctor. He said calmly, "Cassia wants to know if the magic on me will wear off. The magic from the flowers. I died a few hours ago. The flowers brought me back to life."

Dr Morgan dropped the flowers. "Pardon? Say that again. You died?"

Stanley nodded, and then told her about the incident. I was grateful for his explanation as I couldn't get any words out at the moment.

When Stanley had finished talking, the doctor leaned back in her chair and gave Stanley a long studious look. Then her gaze went to me. She said, "That explains your worried face, and your concern about the flowers. Do you need something for your obvious shock?"

I replied, "Blythe has already given me some hot chocolate laced with rum. I'm okay. It's Stanley I'm worried about."

"Of course you are. I am too." She stood up and came over to us. She picked Stanley up. "I'm going to give you a full examination, my little friend. But I can't do it in Brimstone. I don't have the equipment here. Let's step into the human world."

She walked across the room and to a door which had a curtain in front of it. She pulled the curtain back and opened the door which led straight into her office in the human world. It was an exact replica of this one in Brimstone but with the addition of modern technology and equipment. She went through. I was right behind her. I closed the door after us.

Dr Morgan said to me, "I'm going to give Stanley an X-ray first. Then I'll carry out other tests. You can come with us if you want. Or you can use that microscope over there to examine your flowers. I'm assuming you know how to use one?"

I nodded. "I'll stay here and do that." I was on the verge of tears again and needed to compose myself. Why couldn't I stop crying? It was getting ridiculous now.

Stanley waved his paw in goodbye as Dr Morgan took him out of the room.

I went over to the microscope and carefully placed one of the petals between two glass slides. I zoomed in on the slides and focused on the enlarged image, not sure what I was expecting. If there was magic on the petal, I assumed it would have a glow of blue light on it. Or something like that.

I examined the image, frowned and removed the slide. I performed the same procedure three more times using different petals from other flowers. But they all came up with the same result.

The flowers were made up of tiny droplets of liquid. A clear liquid with a blue tinge. The flecks of silver and gold didn't show up in the magnification, which was strange. I zoomed out hoping to see the flecks, but they weren't there.

Dr Morgan returned to the office with Stanley tucked under her arm. She said, "Everything is perfect with this little chap. No bones broken, and not even any signs of healed bones. His heart is as healthy as a kitten's. He's in excellent condition."

Relief flooded me. I smiled at Stanley. He smiled back.

Dr Morgan asked, "What have you discovered about the flowers?" She came over to me with Stanley still in her arms.

I moved to one side and pointed to the slides. "The flowers are made up of droplets of water. Have a look."

She passed Stanley to me and then looked into the microscope. "That is weird. There doesn't seem to be anything holding them together. And where did those flecks of gold and silver go? Let's see what this liquid is made of."

She extracted part of a petal, took it to another area of the office and did something with tubes.

Stanley rested his head against my shoulder and said, "I can feel your worry. But you don't need be worried. I'm okay. Dr Morgan says so."

I stroked his little head. "Did you look at your X-rays?"

He lifted his head. "I did! You should see how many bones I have. It's amazing. I can't wait to tell Oliver about this. It's one adventure after another for me today."

"Yes, I've noticed. Can you stop having adventures? It's not good for my heart." I kissed the top of his head.

"I'll try."

Doctor Morgan called us over. She held a test tube up and said, "This liquid is salt water."

"Like the sea?"

Her look turned solemn. "No. More like tears. These flowers are made from many, many tears."

I took this information in. Then said, "But whose tears?"

Chapter 18

Dr Morgan gave Stanley a cuddle before we left her office. We went straight to Blythe's house to see how she was getting on with the spellbook. And I wanted to let her know about Stanley and the flowers.

We found her in the living room having a chat with Trent.

She stood at our arrival and looked at Stanley. "Get here right now. I want to look at you."

Stanley padded over to her. "I had an X-ray. I could see all my bones. It was awesome! Dr Morgan said I'm in excellent health."

Blythe picked him up and stared into his eyes. Stanley stared back. After a few seconds, she gave him a satisfied nod and declared, "The good doctor is right. You are in perfect health. Could you do me a favour? Trent said you didn't go to the Mooncrest Café. He can't come to Brimstone and miss out on that. Can you take him there now, please? Have anything you want to eat and drink. It's all on me."

It was clear to me she wanted Trent out of the house. It was clear to Stanley too because he said, "Of course. We'll go there now." He jumped out of her arms and landed on Trent's lap. I had no idea he could leap so far. "Trent, you'll love the café. And I'll tell you about my X-ray. Do you know what one is?"

Trent shook his head. "Did it hurt?"

"Not at all. I'll tell you about it on the way. Come on." He jumped off Trent's lap and jogged out of the room. Trent was after him in a flash.

Once we'd heard them leave the house, Blythe beckoned me over to the sofa. She took a seat and said, "I've got something to tell you about Brigid's book."

I sat next to her.

Blythe explained, "While I was talking to Trent, I managed to gather some information about where Brigid has lived over the years. That helped me to break down some of the codes she used according to the towns she was in at that time. She used a mixture of town names and landmarks as substitutes for words." She sighed. "It's going to take me a while to get through the whole book, but I won't give up."

"What have you deciphered so far? Anything useful?"

"I'm not sure about useful, but it is disturbing." She picked up the book and pointed to the first page. "This refers to her early life. It didn't take me long to work these words out. It details Brigid's training as a witch, and the first spells she cast. But as the years progress, her spells change. And not for the better."

A tingle of apprehension ran down my spine. "What did she do?"

"Brigid cast a lot of curses on those creatures who crossed her. She hasn't gone into detail about who crossed her or what they did, but she's given a lot of information about the effects of her curses. She's quite gleeful about the pain she inflicted." Blythe shuddered. "Witches shouldn't use curses, and certainly not for fun. Brigid took great delight in causing pain. Which would have made her many enemies over the years. Who those enemies are, we don't know. But I might find out who they are as I continue to decipher this book."

"Has she written anything about Edie and Avalon? Did they know about her curses?"

"I'm not sure about the curse business, but she has known them for years. There are a few comments about things Edie had told her."

"What kind of things?"

"About the creatures they came across and the things they'd done. You know, like cheating and lying, blackmail and violence. Brigid has written about it in a vague way, as if there aren't any facts to back up Edie's observations. I suspect it's more like gossip than real facts."

I nodded. "What happened to those creatures?"

Blythe gave me a pointed look. "She cast a curse on them. Nasty ones too. If someone had lied, according to Edie, then Brigid would make their tongues disappear so that they could never lie again. And that's just a mild curse compared to the others she performed."

"That's awful. Edie could have been making it all up."

"She could. Some of the residents at the retirement village might have had dealings with Edie and Brigid in the past. They might have decided to now take their revenge."

"What about Avalon? What's her part in this?"

Blythe replied, "I don't know. There are a few comments about the husbands she took on. Brigid didn't like any of them. It sounds like she found a way to get rid of them."

I sighed. "Our list of suspects keeps increasing." I looked at the book. "Anything about the wizards?"

"Not yet."

I said carefully, "This is an awful thing to say, but I don't want to help Brigid, not after what she's done."

"I feel the same, but that's not how we work. We'll have to put our feelings to one side. I'll keep on with this book. Did you find anything out about the flowers?"

I told her what Dr Morgan and I had discovered.

"Tears? I've never come across that before. Of course, that makes you wonder whose tears."

"That's what I'm thinking. And now I know more about Brigid, I'm wondering if they're part of a curse she cast long ago."

Blythe put the book up. "Come with me. I've got some old maps at the back. The retirement village has only been there for about sixty years or so. Let's see what was there before, and if those flowers are mentioned by any chance."

I followed her to a drawer which contained rolls of parchments. Blythe took one out, unrolled it and placed it on the floor. She weighed it down with butterfly-shaped crystals. We got to our knees and examined the area.

Blythe circled part of the map with a pencil. "This is where the village is now. As you can see, it was fields before that. There's no mention of the flowers, but that's not surprising really."

Something caught my attention on the map. "That area. Look at it. It's outside where the village is now. Does it say it's a satyr village?"

Blythe squinted. "It does. That's a large area. There must have been hundreds of satyrs living there. Perhaps they still do. Why are you interested in them?"

"Satyrs work at the village. I've come across a few of them." I quickly told her what the shorts-clad satyr had said to me in the nightclub. I only blushed a little.

Blythe smiled. "They are known for being charming and flirtatious. It could be a coincidence that satyrs work there." She looked at the map again. "But if they've worked there for a while, they might know a lot about Brigid and her enemies. You should talk to them again. Just don't fall for their charms."

"I won't. I'll investigate this area too." I pointed at the satyr village. "There could be satyrs still living there. They could give me more information about the flowers."

"That's a good idea. You do that. I'll get back to Brigid's book. Not that I'm looking forward to that. Don't let Trent know what she's done unless you have to."

As we stood up, Trent came racing into the room. His face was devoid of colour.

"Stanley!" I screamed. "Where is he?"

Stanley ran into the room. "I'm here. I'm still alive. Don't panic."

Trent exclaimed, "It's Grandma! Something terrible had happened." He put his hands on his chest. "I can feel it right here. We have to get back to the village right now!"

Chapter 19

Trent was right to be concerned about his grandma because when we returned to the village and looked at the statues, they had shrunk considerably. The witch figures came up to my knees now. In comparison, the wizard ones looked even bigger.

Trent ran his hands agitatedly through his hair causing it to stick up. He implored, "Do something! Stop them shrinking."

"I don't think I can," I replied helplessly.

"You have to try! Think of something. Anything! Please."

"I can try a protection spell, but I don't know if that would do anything. These are statues made of stone."

Trent grabbed my arm. "But the magic might somehow get to Grandma. You're a witch, and she's a witch, and your magic might connect you somehow. Please, try."

"Okay. I'll give it a go." I brought to mind the protective spells I knew. I cast all of them over the figures, not sure what good it would do.

Trent's eyes were full of desperate tears. "Is there anything else you can do?"

"Yes. We can continue making our enquiries until we find out where your grandma is. I won't stop until I do." I gave him a grim smile. "I promise."

"I promise too," Stanley added. "Do you need a hug, Trent?"

"Yes." Trent's reply was a whisper. He picked Stanley up and pulled him close. Stanley purred.

To take Trent's mind off the shrinking statues, I told him about the blue flowers and what they were made of. After that,

I explained about the ancient map and how satyrs used to live nearby.

Trent's eyes widened. "Satyrs? Loads of them work here. Have you seen them?"

"I've met a few," I confirmed. "But I haven't had a good look around the village yet. Where do they work?"

He looked left and right. "Everywhere. In every building. In all areas." He frowned. "Now that I think about it, no other beings work here. It's all satyrs. That's weird."

"Do you know who owns the village?" I asked.

He shook his head. "Do you think the satyrs know what happened to Grandma?"

Stanley pointed out, "We should talk to those who work in The Fun Zone. That's where my accident happened. One of them must have seen something. Surely."

I hesitated. "I don't really want to go back there. I don't want to put either of you in danger."

Stanley lifted his furry chin. "I'm not afraid of danger. I want Trent to find his grandma as soon as possible."

Trent smiled at him. "When I'm a proper witch, I'm definitely going to get a cat."

They smiled at each other. Whilst I was happy to see them getting along so well, we had work to do.

I said firmly, "We'll talk to that satyr at the gate of The Fun Zone. We don't need to go inside. Come on."

The satyr wasn't much use. I asked him how long he'd been working there, and what he knew about the witches. His replies were a mixture of grunts, shrugs and stares into space. The information I finally got was that he'd worked there for twenty years, he didn't know much about the witches, and couldn't remember the name of whoever owned the village.

He concluded with, "I keep myself to myself. As long as I get paid, I don't care who pays me."

We tried other satyrs as we walked along the village paths. They were all just as useless. I suspected they were acting that way on purpose as some of their replies were very guarded.

One of the last satyrs we spoke to kept glancing nervously towards the clubhouse. I followed his gaze and saw something interesting.

I said thanks and goodbye to the nervous satyr and watched him walk away. When he'd gone, I whispered to Stanley and Trent, "Look at the Mirella Phlox near the clubhouse. It grows thicker around the side of the building. Let's have a closer look."

Making sure no one was watching us, we headed closer to the blue flowers.

Stanley jumped out of Trent's arms and sniffed the flowers. "That's strange. They smell different to the other ones."

"In what way?" I asked.

His whiskers twitched. "You're going to think I'm crazy, but they smell like sadness." His whiskers twitched again. "But there's a hint of happiness too. And love."

I stared at him. "Since when could you smell emotions?"

He grinned. "It must be because I've come back from the dead. Do you remember the movie we saw about that woman who died? When she came back from the dead, she could see ghosts. Maybe I've got a new power now."

Trent's eyes were as wide as saucers. "Can you see ghosts? Where? What do they look like?"

Stanley smiled. "I can't see any ghosts. And I don't want to." His attention went back to the flowers. He buried his nose into them. "Definitely sadness, and a love that's been lost."

I shook my head at my psychic cat. What had happened to him?

Stanley began to move along the side of the clubhouse still inhaling the scent of the plants. "The smell is getting stronger."

Trent and I followed him around the side of the building, along a path behind the structure and towards a wooden fence which was about eight feet high.

Stanley stopped at the fence and looked back at us. "We have to go over the fence. The trail continues over there."

I had no intention of climbing the fence, and there were overhanging branches which prevented us from flying over it. I cast an opening spell on it and a door appeared. I pushed the door open, stepped through and indicated for Trent and Stanley to follow me. Once through, I made the door vanish.

"That was a great spell!" Trent said with a grin. "Can you teach me how to do that?"

"Maybe later." I nodded at Stanley who was already moving away with his nose close to the ground.

Trent frowned. "There aren't any flowers here. What's he smelling?"

We caught up with Stanley and I asked him what he was picking up.

Keeping his nose low, he answered, "It's the same smell. It's getting stronger."

"But there aren't any flowers," Trent pointed out the obvious.

"I know, but their scent is here."

He took us deep into a wooded area. We walked between trees, along a river and over a small stone bridge.

After about fifteen minutes, we came to a clearing where a lone cottage stood. A verandah adorned the front of it. A rocking chair was in front of the only window.

To my horror, Stanley suddenly fell to the ground and began to sob.

I fell to my knees. "Stanley! What's wrong? Tell me."

He shook his head sadly. "My heart is breaking. It hurts. I don't know why. But I do know I have to keep walking." He slowly stood up and walked along the open space in front of us. He headed towards the cottage. We cautiously followed him.

As we got closer to the cottage, the door opened.

A creature stepped out and looked at us.

Chapter 20

The creature was tall and slender. Her long dark hair covered half of her face so it was hard to make out what she looked like. She was wearing a pale green dress which hung to the floor of the small verandah. Even from this distance, I could feel an air of melancholy around her.

Stanley let out a strangled sob and padded towards her. She gave him a surprised look which soon turned to understanding. She picked him up and pressed her cheek gently against his head.

As I moved towards them, I heard her mutter to Stanley, "It's okay. I feel pain too. It's okay. Let it out."

Hating to interrupt this tender moment, I said gently, "Sorry to disturb you."

The creature turned our way and just stared as if not really seeing us.

I held my hand out, "That's Stanley. He's my friend. He led us to you for some reason."

She gave Stanley a loving smile. "It's because we share a deep sadness. A sadness which never fades. Not even with time."

I frowned and took a step closer. "Stanley? Is that how you feel?"

He nodded. "I don't know why, though. I've got nothing to feel sad about. I've got a great life." He looked at the creature. "But I can feel a deep ache in my heart when I'm with you. I must be feeling your pain. I'm sorry it hurts so much."

She stroked his head. "Thank you for caring." She looked at me. "Would you like to stay for a while? I don't have company much. I'm not good at talking, but I'm good at listening. You can tell me exactly how you found me. I'm intrigued."

"Oh, we don't want to disturb you," I lied. I wanted to know who she was, and why Stanley had led us to her.

"You're not disturbing me." She gave Trent a small smile and said to him, "I've got a couple of chairs inside. Would you bring them out, please?"

"Of course." Trent went into the cottage.

She addressed me, "Would you mind if I kept hold of your Stanley for a while? He's got a comforting way about him."

I smiled. "He's a special cat. Keep him as long as you need to."

She walked over to the rocking chair and sat down with Stanley on her knee. Trent came out with two wooden chairs and placed them in front of her. We sat down and looked at the sad creature as she gazed at Stanley. I wasn't sure what to say.

Stanley spoke first. "What's your name? And, if I'm not being too rude, what kind of being are you?"

Her gaze was still soft as she answered. "I'm a woodland nymph. My name is Mirella."

Stanley's ears pricked up. "Mirella? Like the retirement village?"

She frowned. "The retirement village? I don't know of any such place. Is that where you've come from?"

Stanley gave me a confused look.

I took up the questions. "Are you named after a flower? A small blue flower like this one?" I took one from my pocket expecting it to be well and truly flattened by now. But it wasn't.

It remained as fresh as the second I'd picked it. I stood up and placed the flower in Mirella's open palm.

She smiled at the flower. A shaft of sunlight alighted on her hand and caught the gold and silver flecks in it.

A change suddenly came over her. Mirella's eyes widened, and her face turned white. Her hand shook and the flower dropped from it. She threw her head back and let out an ear-piercing scream.

The scream didn't end. It got louder and shriller. Mirella's body shook and her hands clawed at her dress.

Stanley leapt off her knee and ran to me. He said, "What's going on? Why is she screaming like that? Can you do something?"

Before I could think of an appropriate spell, a creature in a dark dress came scuttling across the clearing. It was a female satyr. She was quickly followed by more satyrs of both sexes.

The first satyr shot an angry look my way as she raced onto the verandah and over to Mirella. She put her hands on either side of Mirella's face and gently stroked her cheeks. She muttered, "It's okay now. You are safe. I've got you. It's okay."

Mirella stopped screaming and gave the satyr a blank stare. The satyr continued in a soothing tone. "You are safe. I've got you. You are sleepy now. Sleep. My lovely. Sleep now."

Mirella's eyelids fluttered a little before closing. Her head lolled to one side. The satyr gave a sharp nod to the other satyrs who had gathered around the verandah. A couple of males went over to the sleeping woodland nymph and carefully picked her up. They carried her into the cottage.

Once the door had been closed, the satyr spun around and glowered at us. "Who did this?" she seethed. "Which one of you idiots did this to her?"

"I did," I admitted. "But I didn't mean to upset her."

The satyr marched up to me and jabbed her finger harshly into my shoulder. "You did upset her! And now I've got to help her. I've got to stop those screams of hers. It could take months. Even years like it did the first time." She continued to jab at me. "And all because of you!"

I moved her finger away. "I didn't know that was going to happen to her. If I had, I wouldn't have asked her any questions."

"Questions! You've been asking her questions? What about? Not her past? Don't tell me you did that! How stupid are you? And who gave you permission to be here?"

Despite the fury in her eyes, I stood my ground. "I'm Cassia Winter. I'm a justice witch from Brimstone. I'm investigating the disappearance of residents from the retirement village nearby. My investigation led me here. And to Mirella."

Her eyes narrowed. "What's that village got to do with Mirella?"

I held some blue flowers out. "These flowers are called Mirella Phlox. They grow everywhere in the retirement village, which is also called Mirella."

The satyr peered at the flowers for a few seconds. She looked at me with confusion in her eyes. "There's something familiar about these. Something about the colour, but I can't think what. They grow in the retirement village?"

I nodded. "They don't grow here, but my cat Stanley picked up their scent."

Stanley padded over. "I did. It's very strong. We're sorry for upsetting Mirella. We really didn't mean to. Why did she get so upset? Can we do anything to help her?"

The satyr gave Stanley a small smile. "You can't help her, but thank you. When did she start screaming? Was it something you said to her?"

Stanley nodded his head at the satyr's hand. "It was when she saw the flowers. We really are sorry."

"I can see that," the satyr answered. She gave me a long look. "You think these flowers have something to do with your investigation?"

"I do."

"And you think Mirella in there is connected somehow?"

I nodded.

She let out a heavy sigh. "Then I'd better tell you about her. But I don't want to discuss it here. Mirella is safely asleep in there, and will be for hours. I'll leave someone to sit with her. We'll go to my village." She gave me the flowers back. "I'm Chifia. I've lived in this area for years just as my ancestors have done. Who's that skinny creature behind you?"

"Trent. He's a witch," I explained. "His grandma is one of those who's gone missing. Perhaps you know her? Brigid Sangrey?"

Her nose wrinkled. "Never heard of her. I don't have anything to do with witches. I don't trust them. No offence."

She had a quick word with some nearby satyrs, and then she set off at a brisk pace away from the cottage. She was followed by us and her small army of satyrs who cast suspicious looks in our direction.

Chifia took us through a forest area, over a bridge and to a large clearing. Wooden huts were positioned close to the trees. Circular tables were dotted around a fire which burned brightly despite the warmth of the day. Satyrs of all sizes went about their business, only hesitating a little to stare at us. Some gave Chifia questioning looks, but she dismissed their concerns with a wave of her hand.

She took us to a table nearest to the fire and asked us to sit down. "Let me get you something to drink." She clicked her fingers at a passing satyr and said, "Mint teas over here when you're ready."

The satyr dipped his head and trotted away.

We took a seat at the table. I noticed Trent had pulled Stanley onto his lap. I wasn't sure if he was protecting himself or attempting to keep Stanley safe.

Chifia sat next to me. I asked her, "Are you in charge here?"

She smiled, causing her face to wrinkle. "I am. One of the advantages of getting old. Not that I can control some of the younger ones. They think they know better."

A satyr raced over with a tray. He placed it on the table and said, "Is there anything else? Shall I prepare some food? Or perform a dance? I'm getting better at my jigs now." His eyes were full of hope.

Chifia gave him a kind smile. "Not at the moment. Maybe you can dance for us later. I know how much you've been practising."

He beamed and trotted away with a spring in his hooves.

Chifia passed the mint tea out. "Okay then, Cassia. Ask me what you want. I can't say I'm going to answer all your questions, but you can ask."

I took a quick drink. The tea was incredibly refreshing and made me sit up straighter. I quickly told her about the witches and their disappearance. I pointed out, "There are a lot of satyrs working in the retirement village. Do they come from here?"

"They do. They get paid a decent wage. None of them complain, so I don't have a problem with it." She paused as a thought came to her. "It is just the males who work there. The females have never shown any interest in going there."

"Oh? Why?"

Chifia shrugged. "I don't know." She picked her cup up and took a drink.

"Who employs them?" I asked. "Do you know who owns the village? How do the satyrs find out about the jobs? Do they go for interviews? How do they get paid?"

Chifia gave me a direct look as she lowered her cup. "Do you know how questions work?"

"What do you mean?"

"When you ask someone a question, you're supposed to let them answer it. Once they've done that, you can ask them another question. There's no point firing a million questions at me all at once. Is there?"

Heat came to my cheeks. "Sorry. I can't help it sometimes."

She tutted and shook her head. "That's the problem with youth. You're always in a rush. Why is that?"

Trent ventured nervously, "We are in a rush. My grandma could die." He explained about the shrinking statues and what that meant.

Chifia's eyes widened. Then she gave me a withering look. "Why didn't you say that to begin with? What was your first question?"

"Who employs your satyrs?" I asked.

"No idea. Next question."

"Do you know who owns the retirement village?"

"No. Next question." Her look was intense which made me shift in my seat. I don't even think she blinked as she stared at me.

"Erm, how do they find out about the jobs?"

"Ah. I do know the answer to that one. The jobs are posted on the trees. No one knows who puts them there, before you ask. And that's how they get paid too. Their wages are pinned on the trees with a name on the envelope."

Stanley said, "Really? And no one steals their wages?"

Chifia gave Stanley a confused look. "Steals their wages? Why would anyone do that? Is that what happens where you've come from? Is it full of thieves? Is theft common in your world? What else goes on?"

Not missing a beat, Stanley said innocently, "Sorry? What was your first question again? You fired too many at me then."

Chifia burst into laughter. "I deserved that!"

Stanley chuckled. "Sorry. I couldn't help it. Can you tell us about Mirella, please?"

Chifia took another drink of her tea before beginning. "I told you earlier that I've lived here for years. It must have been about fifty years ago when I first saw Mirella. No. Just a moment. Let me think. It was sixty years ago. Anyway. I was sitting here with my parents when the earth began to shake. The most awful shrieking noise pierced the air. It went right to my very bones. We all went rushing towards the noise and found Mirella on her knees in that area where she lives now. It was part of the forest back then. The poor creature was wailing and screaming as if her heart was being torn out."

She paused as tears came to her eyes. My eyes began to sting too.

Chifia continued, "We couldn't calm her down. How she continued to make that noise, I don't know. But she did. We checked her for injuries, but found nothing. Whatever was hurting her was on the inside. My mother finally calmed her down by giving her a special tea and stroking her hair. After a while, Mirella stopped screaming and fell asleep."

"What was in the tea?" I asked.

"Does that matter?" Chifia asked.

"No. Sorry." I gave my mint tea a dubious look.

The sharp-eyed satyr caught my look. "It wasn't that mint tea. Do you want to hear about Mirella?"

I gave her a nod.

"We brought Mirella back to our village and put her in my parents' bed. Every time she woke up, she began to scream. So Mother kept giving her tea and saying soothing words. We knew Mirella was a nymph, so we tried to find out where she'd come from, and if she had any family to help her. But no one knew of her. We couldn't send her away in her state, so she stayed with us. It took months before she stopped waking up and screaming. Then another few years before she talked. She'd been silent for so long that we all thought she couldn't talk."

"What did she say?" Stanley asked.

Chifia's small smile was full of sadness. "Not much. She didn't know why she was in this area, or why she was screaming. She said there was a pain in her heart and screaming made it better. By this time, we'd grown fond of Mirella and didn't want her to leave. She felt the same but insisted on living away from us. She didn't want her sadness to affect us. We helped her build that cottage, and we keep checking on her. She hasn't had a screaming fit for decades. Until now."

There was a heavy silence.

I broke it. "I am so very sorry. But I..." My voice trailed off.

Chifia said, "You still want to talk to her about those flowers?"

"I do. But I won't. Not if it's going to cause her pain." I looked around us. "Perhaps I can speak to some of the males who work in the village."

I felt a presence behind me. A soft voice whispered in my ear. "I knew we'd meet again, my one true love."

Chapter 21

It was the satyr from The Howling Werewolf nightclub. He slid into the seat next to me and placed an impossibly hot hand over mine. He was still wearing his gold shorts and nothing else. He gazed into my eyes and muttered, "We are meant to be together. Can you feel how much my heart beats just for you?" He grabbed my hand and placed it over his chest. "Can you feel our love echoed in the beats of our hearts? Beating as one."

All I could feel was an unpleasant warmth. And not just in him. My cheeks were aflame and so were my ears, neck and forehead. I didn't know I could blush in so many places. With some effort, I pulled my hand free and announced, "I can't feel anything."

His eyes glittered with mischief. "We must run away together right now, my beautiful Cassia. I can't wait for our life together to begin." His glance went to something behind me. "What's wrong with that cat?"

I spun around in horror, expecting Stanley to have expired again. To my utter relief, he was still alive. He was more than alive. He was bristling with rage as he stood on the table, his back arched and his tail straight as a poker.

He hissed at the satyr, "Back away from Cassia right now before I hurt you."

I blinked. I'd never heard Stanley sound so angry. I said, "It's okay, Stanley. I can handle this."

Foolishly, the satyr put his arm around my shoulder and said, "You can't hurt me, cat. And you can't stop the love between Cassia and me. No one can."

"We'll see about that," Stanley muttered darkly. He leapt forward.

My hands shot out and I caught my flying cat. I pulled him close. "Stanley? What's got into you?"

He tried to get free, but I had a firm hold on him. After a few moments, he went limp, lowered his head and mumbled, "I'm so sorry. I don't know what came over me."

"It's okay." I gave the satyr a pointed look. "Move your hand from my shoulder right now."

The satyr's said softly, "Nothing can come between us. No one can stop our love."

He was suddenly yanked to his feet by Chifia. The surprised satyr held his hands up in defence. "Chifia! I didn't see you there."

Chifia was a few feet smaller than the satyr but she seemed to take up more space. She snapped, "Yes, Vrathix, I know you didn't see me there but I certainly saw you! And I'm seeing much more of you than I want to. What did I tell you about wearing those shorts?"

He withered under her intense look. "You told me not to wear them."

"And have you been to work looking like that?"

His answer was a meek nod.

She threw her hands up in disgust. "I don't know what I'm going to do with you, I just don't. It's bad enough that you're wearing something so skimpy, but putting your hands all over my guest is inexcusable!"

Vrathix shot a look my way. "But we're in love. Tell her, my Cassia."

"We are not in love," I informed him firmly.

"But we are," he insisted. "You just don't know it yet."

Chifia poked his shoulder. "She knows her own mind. And even if she was foolish enough to fall for you, you know nothing could come of it. You know our rules about mixing with other species. You know it can never happen. Not after what happened in the past." She added a couple of pokes to confirm her words.

Vrathix glowered at her and rubbed his shoulder. "I know the rules. But I don't know why we have them. No one does. No one can remember what happened in the past. It's a lie to scare us, and to make sure we never leave this village."

Chifia pressed her lips together and looked Vrathix over in disgust. She said sharply, "How can you say that? It's not a lie. We old ones know exactly what happened."

"Yeah? Then why can't you ever tell us? You say something terrible occurred, and then you never tell us what it was."

Chifia wagged a finger at him. "I'll tell you right now! It—" She abruptly stopped and lowered her finger. "I can't remember what happened. But I know something did. I'm sure of it."

Vrathix shook his head sadly. "See? This always happens. You threaten us about something terrible which once happened between two different species. But then you never tell us what it was."

The older satyr said, "It was just on the tip of my tongue." She stared at the ground as if hoping to find the answer there. Her head snapped up. "This doesn't excuse your behaviour! Or those shorts. Go and get changed into something decent."

Vrathix looked my way, blew me a kiss and said, "I will return, my love. Don't go anywhere." He turned around and sauntered away.

Chifia shook her head at him. "The youth are too free with their emotions. I apologise. Once they fall in love, all common sense leaves their minds." Her attention went briefly to Stanley and then back to me. "I assume you've got the same problem with your young cat here. I saw how quick he was to anger."

Stanley said quietly, "I'm sorry. That wasn't like me at all. And I'm not that young for a cat."

The satyr tipped her head to one side. "Really? You move like a young cat."

Stanley let out a quiet whimper which I only just caught. What was wrong with him?

I stood up and said, "We'll leave now. I can talk to some of your satyrs at the village. Although, they weren't much use the first time I talked to them."

"Weren't they?" Chifia asked. "When you go back, tell them you've talked to me. And if that doesn't convince them to open their mouths, then you come back here and get me. I'll soon sort them out."

I smiled. "I'm sure you would. Thank you." I hesitated. "Is there anything I can do for Mirella?"

"No. Leave her to us. We know what to do."

We said goodbye to Chifia and headed back to the village. Trent carried both our broomsticks as I was still holding Stanley.

Once we were through the fence via my door spell, I said to Stanley, "What's wrong with you?"

His eyes were full of fear. "I've gone to the dark side."

"What do you mean? What dark side?"

"The dark side where evil cats go." He shuddered. "I can feel the evil inside me."

I heard a rumble coming from his stomach. "You're just hungry. There's nothing wrong with you."

He put his paws on my face. "You have to listen to me. You saw how angry I got at that cheeky satyr. I couldn't control myself. Do you remember that film we saw about animals coming back to life? How evil they were?" His eyes went wide. "That's me! I'm turning evil. My sinister side is taking over. My heart is turning black. You're not safe."

I looked into his little face. "Stanley Winter, you don't have an evil bone in your body. If you were truly turning into a fiendish feline, would you warn me about it?"

"Oh. I don't suppose I would. But I'm new to this wicked way of life."

I shook my head at him. "I don't think you're becoming evil. Those flowers have made you younger. I've seen how full of energy you are. Chifia saw it too. And Dr Morgan."

"Younger? Do you think so?" He smiled. "I like the sound of that."

A sudden sour aroma made me gag.

Trent's head turned to the right. "It's Creg! He's near. Come on. We have to talk to him!" He ran off with my broomstick still in his hand.

Stanley jumped out of my arms, somersaulted in the air and landed safely on all four paws. He yelled, "I'm right behind you!" He sped off.

I sighed. Having a younger Stanley was making me feel old. I had no option but to jog after them. I wanted to talk to Creg too. He would know who owned this village. He might even know why the Mirella Phlox grew here and nowhere else.

As I jogged around the clubhouse and towards the line of statues, I came to a sudden stop.

I hadn't been expecting that.

Chapter 22

Creg was standing a few feet away from the wizard statues with his thick arms folded over his chest. He was glaring at the two creatures who were jumping from side to side in front of him with their fists jabbing in his direction. Well, paws not fists for one of the creatures.

I yelled, "Trent! Stanley! Stop that immediately!"

Trent waved his skinny fist at Creg. "He knows something! He must do. I'm going to get the truth out of him even if I have to force it out."

Creg looked as if he could knock Trent over with a hearty exhale. And that's just what he did. He took a deep breath and exhaled. I caught the back end of the stench which made my nose want to run away. Trent got the full blast of it. He retched, leaned over and made gagging noises. Creg raised a bushy eyebrow at Stanley. My brave cat ran over to me and leapt into my arms.

I said to Creg, "I'm so sorry. I don't know what's got into them." I gave Stanley a hard look. "You know better."

Stanley dipped his head in embarrassment. I heard a quiet apology coming from him.

"You should control your pets," Creg snarled. He waved his arm over the witch figures. "Look at what that skinny one has done to these statues! He's made them smaller. It's vandalism. He's going to pay for it."

Trent's green face turned Creg's way. He straightened up. "I didn't do anything to them. It's those wizards. They've done something to my grandma. You should throw them out of the village."

Creg's look darkened. "I know who I'm going to throw out of the village, and it's not a wizard." He advanced on Trent.

Balancing Stanley in one arm, I held my free hand up ready to cast a spell if needed. "Don't you touch him! He didn't do anything to these figures."

Creg rounded on me. "Oh yeah? Have you got proof?"

I quickly considered that. "No. Not proof. But I trust Trent. He wouldn't do such a thing."

"Are you sure about that?"

Trent cried out, "I didn't! Why would I?"

Creg gave him a dark look which lasted for about three seconds. Then he said, "You want your grandma out of the way."

"No, I don't! I love her." Trent was no match for Creg's glower, but he had a go anyway.

I asked, "Why would Trent want his grandma out of the way?"

Trent began to bluster his outrage, but I held my hand in his direction as a warning to keep quiet.

Creg looked at me now. "Once his grandma is out of the way, then he gets the retirement village." He took in my stunned silence, then clarified the matter. "Brigid Sangrey owns the Mirella Retirement Village. She has done since it was first opened. But she doesn't want anyone to know. Especially her witch friends. Probably doesn't trust them."

Trent stared at Creg. "You're lying. Grandma would have told me."

Creg's thick bushy eyebrows rose. My stomach clenched as I saw something scuttle out of them. Creg said, "I think she did tell you. And you want the village now. You can't wait till she dies of old age. You're too impatient for that."

Creg had a point about Trent's impatience, but I didn't voice my agreement.

Trent sank to the ground and wrapped his arms around himself. "She didn't tell me. Why didn't she? I wouldn't have told anyone. Didn't she trust me?"

Creg studied Trent as if deciding whether to believe him or not. Creg said to me, "Have you found out where Brigid is yet? I'm having to run this village on my own. As if I haven't got enough to do."

"I'm still making enquiries." My glance alighted on the blue flowers near the witch statues. I pointed at them and asked Creg, "Why are there so many of these?"

He shrugged. "They're Brigid's idea. She's the one who made them appear. Get everywhere, they do."

I frowned. "But why these?"

He shrugged again. Dirt fell from his jumper. "I think it's something to do with her past. I heard her talking about it once to that noisy friend of hers. That one who's always out late. You should ask her ex-husband about it."

"Her ex-husband? Whose? Brigid's? I didn't know she'd been married."

Creg shook his head. "No, the other one." He pointed to Avalon. "Talk to her ex-husband. He's a wizard." His finger moved along the line. "That one there is her ex."

Without looking at where he was indicating, I replied, "We have spoken to Meevan. I found him in one of the nightclubs singing about his past love."

Stanley said, "Cassia, he's not pointing at Meevan. He's pointing at Arestrum. Look."

I did so. Stanley was right. I asked Creg, "Do you mean Arestrum?"

"That's the one. Keeps calling himself Arestrum The Great. I'm not calling him that. He's not great at all."

"Hang on," I said. "Was Avalon married to Meevan and Arestrum?"

Creg gave me an incredulous look. "Yes. You're slow on the uptake. No wonder you haven't found those witches yet. If you don't find them soon, I'll look for them myself." He ended his comments with a filthy look at Trent. Then he stormed away. His aroma took a while to go with him.

I put Stanley down and helped Trent to his feet. In a stern voice, I said, "No more running away. No more confrontations. Got that?"

He gave me a feeble nod.

I turned to Stanley. "The same goes for you."

"I'm very sorry, Cassia," Stanley said. "I love you."

My mouth twitched in readiness for a smile. I said gruffly, "I know. I love you too. Let's find Arestrum and see what he's got to say about Avalon."

I picked up my discarded broomstick and set off towards the clearing where we'd found him telling stories earlier. Trent and Stanley walked silently behind me.

As we approached the clearing, I heard the sad wail of someone singing about the loss of their loved one.

I sighed. Not Meevan again? I couldn't bear to listen to his tuneless warble.

But it wasn't Meevan who was singing.

Chapter 23

Arestrum was sitting in Brigid's chair, exactly where we'd found him before. He crooned sadly to himself in the empty clearing.

Stanley, Trent and I halted by the trees for a few seconds. I held my hand up to Trent who looked as if he was going to rush towards the wizard. I whispered, "Let's hear what he's singing about."

Arestrum sang.

We listened.

He wailed about losing the love of his life. His voice turned bitter as he recalled the evil witch who had come between them. His song concluded with him getting revenge on the interfering witch. When he'd finished, he placed his hands on his lap and a small smile flitted over his lips.

We'd heard enough.

I moved towards Arestrum and said, "That was an interesting song. Was it about Avalon?"

"What? Where did you come from?" His glance alighted on Stanley. "He's alright then."

"Yes, he's fine." I gave him a long look. Was he annoyed Stanley was still alive? "You didn't tell us you'd been married to Avalon."

He looked down at his cloak. "You didn't ask me about Avalon."

"I certainly did!" I replied. "You said you barely spoke to her. Why did you lie to me?"

He raised his eyes to meet mine. "It was easier. It's hard for me to talk about my true feelings for Avalon. It's too painful. Anyway, I don't see what it's got to do with you."

"It's important information!" I took a moment to control my temper. "That song you were singing, is the evil witch Brigid? Please don't lie to me."

His look darkened. "Yes. Brigid convinced Avalon to end our marriage. She probably used magic. Dark magic."

I shook my head at him. "You told me earlier that you had respect for Brigid. That's not true is it?"

"No. How could I respect such an evil being who only thought of herself and would use whatever means necessary to get what she wanted? I hate her. I'm glad she's gone. I hope she never comes back."

"Did you get rid of her?"

His expression brightened a little. "I wish I had. I'd be a hero around here if I was responsible for that. She scared the residents, you know. But no one would stand up to her."

"I've heard that from another wizard," I said. "I also know Avalon was married to a friend of yours. Did you know about each other's marriages?"

"We did. But our love for Avalon never affected our friendship."

I wasn't so sure about that, but I didn't pursue it. Something else he'd just said needed clarifying. I asked, "What did you mean about Brigid getting what she wanted?"

I could feel Trent right behind me. He was going to hear things about his grandma which he wouldn't like. But I couldn't protect him much longer. Much as I didn't want him to get hurt, the truth was coming out.

Arestrum said, "Brigid made sure she and the other witches got the best accommodation. And she had her statue placed at the front of the line. She went to every residents' meeting and if she didn't like what someone was saying, then she made it clear they were in the wrong. Soon after, that particular resident would have changed their minds about their previous comments. And when that resident met Brigid around the village, it was clear they were scared of her. Some of them even left the village."

"What do you think she did to them?" I asked.

"Use your imagination. My guess is that she used magic to torment them. She's supposed to be retired, but she kept saying witches never retire. I saw her using magic on many an occasion. Every day, in fact."

I glanced over my shoulder at Trent. I had expected an outburst from him by now, but he was silent. His attention was on the ground.

I tapped Trent on the shoulder. "Have you anything to say about this? Did you know your grandma was using magic every day?"

He looked at me and nodded. "She told me not to tell anyone. Residents did seem to be frightened of her, though. I thought it was because they were so impressed with what she'd done in the past." He looked towards the wizard. "I don't think she would actually hurt anyone. Not Grandma."

"She did hurt residents!" Arestrum declared. "And someone around here decided they wouldn't be intimidated by Brigid any longer. They got rid of her. But why did they have to get rid of Avalon too? That's what I don't understand."

"And Edie," I added. "She's gone too."

"Oh, yes. I keep forgetting about her."

I pointed to a nearby patch of flowers. "What do you know about them?"

He regarded the plants. "They are flowers. They're blue flowers. And they grow in this village and nowhere else." He gave me an expectant look. "What were you expecting me to say?"

"Do you know if Brigid brought them here? Creg said she did, and that they've got something to do with her past."

The wizard's brow furrowed. "Her past? That's interesting. I'd almost forgotten about that incident." He nodded to himself.

"What incident?" I prompted.

"Avalon mentioned it to me while we were still married. She had a big fall-out with Brigid years ago. She refused to go into details, but I could tell it was something huge. Brigid eventually forgave Avalon, and they've remained friends ever since." He sat up straighter. "But I did wonder if Brigid had forgiven Avalon for whatever she'd done. I'd sometimes catch Brigid staring at Avalon in a strange, thoughtful kind of way. Almost as if she was plotting something."

"Do you know when this argument happened?"

He mulled the matter over for a few seconds. "About sixty years ago. I think that's what she said."

I took a sharp intake of breath and shared a look with Stanley.

Stanley said, "That's when Mirella first started screaming. This can't be a coincidence."

"Mirella?" Arestrum asked. "Who's that? Another witch?"

"No," I told him. "She's a woodland nymph."

"Oh? And she's got the same name as those flowers? And the village? That is strange." He addressed Stanley. "What was that you said about her screaming?"

Stanley shot me a questioning look. I gave him a nod. Stanley said, "Something happened to her sixty years ago which caused her to start screaming in pain. But it's her heart which is hurting, not anything on the outside."

The wizard's eyebrows rose. "This must have something to do with Brigid. It sounds like something she would do. I wonder what it was? I wonder if it's the nymph who's now got her revenge on Brigid? Good for her."

The same thoughts were going through my mind. Despite what had happened when we'd last spoke to Mirella, I knew we would have to speak to her again.

Something yellow fluttered in front of us and gently landed on Stanley's nose. It was a Brimstone butterfly. These wonderful creatures carried messages in written or audible form.

Stanley went cross-eyed looking at the butterfly's open wings and said, "There's a message from Blythe. She wants us to go back to Brimstone straight away. She's got some urgent information for you, Cassia."

I held my hand out and the butterfly landed on my open palm. "Please tell Blythe we're on our way." The butterfly flapped his wings to acknowledge my message and then flew away.

"Wow," Trent's voice was full of awe. "I didn't know they could do that."

I said to Trent, "Do you want to come with us back to Brimstone?" My look softened. "But I must warn you, Blythe could have some unpleasant information about your grandma."

There was a sadness in Trent's eyes. It didn't suit his young face. He said, "I want to know more about Grandma. And I'll just have to deal with what I find out."

"Okay. We'll go now." I looked at Arestrum. "Is there anything else you want to tell us? Any other important information you've kept from us?"

His look was indignant. "There's no need to be like that." He glanced at Stanley. "I am glad your cat is okay."

Stanley padded over to him. "Did you try to kill me? You were in that area. We saw you."

Arestrum blanched. "I was there. I was looking in vain for Avalon. But I didn't try to kill you. I would never do that."

"You accused me of doing it," Trent said.

"Yes. I know. I apologise. I was lashing out. But I didn't see what happened, and I thought if you were anything like your grandma, then you wouldn't think twice about hurting..." He fell silent obviously not wanting to go into details.

I beckoned Stanley back to me. "Let's go. I don't want to be in this village for a moment longer."

We left Mirella Retirement Village at top speed. Dark secrets from the past were affecting the present. And Brigid's spellbook could help us unravel this mystery. I had a feeling Trent's illusions about his grandma were going to be well and truly shattered.

As we approached Brimstone, a very welcome sight met us.

Chapter 24

Luca, a guardian of Brimstone was standing at the end of Blythe's path. He was also my boyfriend, which is why I ran into his open arms as soon as we landed. Sometimes, I just needed a big hug.

I gazed into his lovely blue eyes and said, "Hi."

"Hi yourself." He kissed me. "You look troubled. And I know why. Blythe's told me about your latest investigation. I'm assuming that's Trent behind you talking to Stanley."

"It is."

Luca sent a smile Trent's way. He lowered his voice to a whisper. "Blythe's got some information for you about Brigid. But she doesn't want Trent to hear it. Not yet. I'll keep an eye on him." He kissed me again and released me.

That hug wasn't nearly long enough. But I had work to do. I watched Luca as he picked Stanley up and tickled him under the chin. Had Blythe told him about Stanley's accident? I'd already decided I was going to refer to it as an accident from now on.

Trent was giving Luca a bashful smile. I moved closer to hear what they were saying.

Luca said to Trent, "I'm pleased to meet you, Trent. Have you had a look around Brimstone yet?"

"Yes. Stanley showed me."

"Ah, but did he show you the secret streets and the hidden alleyways?"

"No. He didn't."

Stanley patted Luca's shoulder. "I don't know about those places. Why haven't you mentioned them before?"

Luca grinned. "I can show you them now. And I'll show Trent too." He looked at the young witch. "If you want to come with me? I'll introduce you to some of the other guardians in Brimstone. Did you know we're shapeshifters? Well, most of us."

Trent's mouth fell open. He gulped and said, "Shapeshifters? Really?"

Luca nodded. He glanced upwards. "It's getting dark. Why don't you stay at my apartment tonight, Trent? I'll get the other guardians around and make a night of it." He noticed my stern look. "Not a late night, obviously."

Trent clasped his hands together gleefully. "I would love that. Thank you. Thank you so much."

"You're welcome. Stanley, are you coming with us?"

Stanley gave me a quick look before answering. "No. I'll stay with Cassia. She's worried about me."

"She's always worried about you," Luca said with a smile.

Stanley said, "But she's got a good reason this time." He craned his head so he was on level with Luca's ear. Then he whispered something.

By the look of utter horror on Luca's face, I guessed Stanley was telling him about the accident. When Stanley had finished, Luca was several shades paler and there were tears in his eyes.

Stanley said, "I'm totally fine. Better than fine. I feel younger and I've got loads of energy. Watch this." He flipped himself out of Luca's arms, landed on the ground and performed two pirouettes on his back legs. He bowed and then ran over to me.

"Show-off," I muttered with a smile.

Stanley chuckled.

Luca was still pale. I was now grateful for Trent's impatient ways because he was firing question after question at Luca. Luca blinked at Trent, nodded and said, "Yes. We can do that. Come on." He gave me a look full of concern before walking away with the chattering young man.

We found Blythe sitting on the carpet in her living room. Pieces of paper were spread out in front of her. She pointed to me and asked, "How are you?"

"I'm fine," I said heavily. "Tired. Confused. But fine."

She pointed to Stanley. "And you?"

"I'm marvellous," he said. "I feel better than I ever have. How are you?" He padded over to her and sat at her side.

Blythe stroked Stanley's head. "I'm all the better for seeing you."

I propped my broomstick against the wall and joined them on the carpet. I asked, "Are these pages from Brigid's book? Have you taken it apart?"

"I had to. There were words written at the very edges of the pages near the spine. I've managed to decode most of her words. It's not good. Brigid has done things which turn my stomach. I can't even bear to repeat them. You can read those pages later, if you really want to." She held up a small piece of torn paper. "This was all that was left in the middle of the book. Brigid did something which she didn't want to remember. Or something so evil that she didn't want anyone to know about it if they ever broke her code."

I looked at the paper. "How can that help us?"

Blythe smiled. "I can do a spell which can bring the full page back to us. But only for a second or two. And then it'll be gone. I wanted you here to see the page when it appears. And you can take a photo with that phone of yours. I'm not sure it'll pick up the image of a magical page, but we can try."

I took my phone out. "I'm ready."

Stanley said, "I'm nervous. What are we going to find out? Is anyone else nervous?"

I nodded.

Blythe said, "I'm too angry at Brigid to be nervous. I want to know exactly what she's done." She took a deep breath and held the bit of paper up. "Okay. Here goes."

She closed her eyes and muttered something which seemed to be in another language.

Stanley gasped as the scrap of paper began to grow. He whispered, "It's working."

I was mesmerised by the magic for a moment. Then I came to my senses and aimed my phone at the thing in front of me. Even though the page wasn't its full size yet, I began to take photos.

Within five seconds, the page was the same size as the others scattered on the carpet. Even though there was a blue light surrounding the page, I could make out lines of writing.

Blythe opened her eyes and looked at the words. There was a flash of blue and the paper disappeared. Not even the original scrap remained.

Blythe turned desperate eyes my way. "Did you read it? Did you get a photo? It was gone too quickly for me to make any sense of it."

I sent a silent wish before looking at my phone. Despite taking half a dozen photos, only one remained. "I've only got one image. And it's just half a page."

"It's better than nothing," Blythe pointed out. "Let me have a look."

I shuffled closer to Blythe and we read the words together. Most of them were in code, so I didn't get very far with it.

When we'd finished reading Brigid's words, I said to Blythe, "I can only make out a few words. Maple Glade. Is that the name of a village?"

Blythe nodded. "It's where woodland nymphs live." She frowned as she looked at my phone again. "According to the date, something happened there sixty years ago. Something which caused Brigid to cast spells before abruptly leaving the village. I've seen those coded names in other parts of her book. I'll be able to tell you soon which spells she used." She looked at the scattered pages. "It might take a while as I'll have to go through these again."

"I'll help," I offered.

"Cassia, you're worn out," Blythe said. "You need to sleep. Stay here for the night. I'll work on this."

"And I'll help," Stanley said. "I'm wide awake."

I shook my head. "I don't think I could sleep. I've got too much going on in my head."

Blythe gently tucked my hair behind my ears. She muttered something which I didn't catch. Then I slowly fell to the carpet, my eyes suddenly too heavy for me to keep open. I fell into a welcome darkness.

Chapter 25

I woke up the next morning in a strange bed with Stanley next to me.

He nuzzled his head next to mine and said, "Morning. You've been asleep all night."

I pulled him close. "Have I? Where am I?"

"In one of Blythe's spare bedrooms. She put you here last night. And she used magic to change you into some pyjamas." He chuckled. "They've got cats on them."

I smiled as I looked at the creatures on my sleeve. "I think Blythe cast a sleeping spell on me."

"She did. But you needed it. How do you feel?"

"Annoyed about the sleeping spell. But I do feel rested. And ready for action." My stomach growled. "As soon as I've had something to eat. Shall we go to the café?"

"There's no need. Blythe has prepared something for you." He moved to the end of the bed and aimed his paw at a covered dish on the table. "There's eggs, bacon, sausages, toast and hash browns. And tea, of course."

I sat up and reached for the tray. "I'm not sure I'll manage it all," I lied unconvincingly. "How are you today?"

"I feel fabulous." He strutted across the blanket. "I haven't got a single ache or pain in my body. I've been up most of the night with Blythe, but I don't feel at all tired."

I picked up a piece of toast and ate it while keeping my eyes on Stanley. I didn't want to voice my worries, but that didn't stop me from thinking them.

I didn't need to tell Stanley what I was thinking because he said, "I know what's going on in your mind. And you can stop it. I'm totally fine. Blythe examined me again last night. And Dr Morgan came round and did the same. Did you want to know what's been going on whilst you've been in the land of Nod?"

I poured myself a cup of tea. "Yes, please."

He settled himself next to me. "Do you remember the name of that town where the woodland nymphs live?"

"Maple Glade?"

"That's the one. Luca called into Blythe's last night and she told him what we'd found out. He's been through that village a few times and he knows of a nymph who's lived there for a long time. He said if something happened there sixty years ago, then she would know. He gave us her name."

I nodded, my mouth full of scrambled egg.

"Blythe asked Luca to keep Trent with him while we get on with our investigation."

I swallowed the egg. "Why?"

"She doesn't want him getting in our way, especially when the truth about Brigid comes out. I told her how he keeps rushing into danger, and how you have to keep chasing after him."

"And did you tell Blythe how you tried to have a fight with Creg?"

He gave me a grin. "I did. She laughed and said I needed to control my youthful spirit. She's worked out some of the spells Brigid used sixty years ago, those ones which we saw on the torn paper."

I placed some egg, bacon and sausage on a piece of toast. "Go on."

"One of the spells was a, oh, now what was it?" He tapped his furry chin. He broke into a smile. "It was a forgetting one."

"Are you trying to make a joke, Stanley?" I shoved the laden toast into my mouth.

He nodded. "I thought that was a good one. Another spell was a youth one. It was to keep someone frozen in time. Not like they can't move, but like their body won't age."

I frowned. "That sounds like a nice spell."

"That's what I said to Blythe. But she said it could be a curse if all your friends and family age and you don't. She said there must be more to it than a simple youth spell." He looked over his shoulder and lowered his voice. "Blythe keeps herself looking young, and so does the doctor. No one minds about that."

I considered the matter. "They live here in Brimstone where magic is everywhere. But imagine if I stayed young-looking in the human world. People would become suspicious, even jealous. And I wouldn't want to look young forever."

Stanley gave me a kind look. "You look beautiful whatever your age. Even when you're old and wrinkly, I'll still love you."

"Thanks." I paused. "Mirella looks young even though she's over sixty years old. I wonder if woodland nymphs don't age and that's normal?"

"We'll find out when we visit that other nymph," Stanley pointed out. "But Blythe said Brigid could have cast a youth spell on Mirella for some reason. And we think Edie might have used the forgetting spell on herself. Everyone keeps forgetting who she is, don't they?"

"That's right. Unless Brigid cast the spell on Edie for some reason. Maybe to forget the awful thing Brigid did to Mirella.

And maybe the spell worked too well and now everyone keeps forgetting Edie."

Stanley sighed. "This is making me feel tired."

"Where's your youthful energy?" I teased. "Don't give up on me now. We've got lots to do. Have you had your breakfast?"

"I've had three. I'm hungry all the time." He stood on his hind legs and turned from side to side. "Do I look as if I'm putting on weight?"

"No. You look just the same. Did Blythe find any other spells from that torn paper?"

Stanley sat down. "She did. But she doesn't know what spell it is. It was the last one on the paper, and only half of it was on there. She's working on it now."

"Okay. Is that everything you've found out?"

"It is. Are we ready to go?"

"I thought you were tired."

"That was a minute ago. I'm raring to go." He leapt off the bed the ran over to the door.

"Stanley, I'm not going out in my pyjamas. And I need a shower. Give me twenty minutes. I'll meet you downstairs."

Blythe met me at the front door twenty minutes later with details on the woodland nymph and where the village was. She looked tired. And worried.

She said, "Cassia, be careful. If Brigid and the others are still alive, they won't appreciate you digging into their past. And it's a dark and murky past. As soon as I find out what that other spell is, I'll let you know."

Stanley and I left her house and took to the skies.

Stanley looked over his shoulder at me and said, "You're worried about what we're going to find out, aren't you? Me too. And I'm a bit scared. I hope we don't bump into Brigid. I've never met her, but she sounds terrifying."

I gave him a grim look. "She sounds evil. We've dealt with evil beings before. We're going to find out what she did sixty years ago. No matter how awful it was."

Chapter 26

As soon as we landed in Maple Glade, I was reminded of something. I said to Stanley, "Look at all the tree houses. And the walkways connecting them. Doesn't it look like The Forest Zone at the retirement village?"

He nodded. "I was thinking the same thing. Brigid must have based that area on this village." He looked left and right. "Where is everyone?"

I glanced upwards. "Probably in their homes. Let's fly to the nearest one and start asking questions." When I looked back at Stanley, he was halfway up a tree. I had never seen him climb a tree before.

A movement in the bushes caught my attention. I could feel someone looking my way. I took a few steps towards the bush and called out, "Hello? Is someone there? I'm Cassia Winter. And that's my cat scrambling up a tree behind me. Hello?"

A creature stepped shyly from the bushes. She looked similar in build to Mirella, so I assumed she was a woodland nymph. Her long hair covered half of her face, but it didn't mask the sadness in her eyes. I had seen that very look on Mirella yesterday. This nymph had a look of Mirella about her, but she was much older. Wrinkles lined her face and her back was stooped. She gave me a small smile and came over to me.

"Are you a witch? You look like one." There was worry in her voice, and a hint of fear. "We don't welcome witches here, not after what happened. Are you going to hurt us?"

"No," I said gently. "But I would like to talk about some witches who have gone missing. Would it be okay if I talked to you?"

She glanced upwards. "Will your cat hurt me? I don't like cats."

"Stanley would never hurt anyone. He's a gentle cat." I pushed the image of Stanley jabbing his paws at Creg firmly from my mind. I aimed a call upwards. "Stanley, come down. Now, please."

I yelped as he suddenly appeared on the grass next to me. He said, "Did you see that? I jumped from the highest branch. Just like a superhero."

I shook my head at him. I would be having words with him later. I said to the nymph, "He's not normally like this. Can I have your name?"

"It's Nemea." Her voice was meek and quiet. "Are there any other witches with you?"

"No. It's just me and Stanley." I smiled. "Actually, we were looking for you. My friend Luca gave us your name. He said you've lived in Maple Glade for a long time."

Her expression brightened. "Luca? He's a trusted friend here. Are you friends of his?"

Stanley said, "We're very close friends. We love him." He took a careful step forward. "I hope you don't mind me saying this, but you look sad. Do you need a hug?"

She swiftly took a step back. "Don't touch me!"

Stanley backed up. "I'm sorry. I didn't mean to upset you."

Nemea sighed. "No, I'm sorry. I'm judging you based on my past. I had a bad experience with a witch's cat. He was called

Edward." She swallowed as if fighting to say her next words. "He belonged to a witch called Brigid Sangrey."

I stared at Nemea. "Brigid Sangrey? Are you sure about that?"

She nodded nervously. "I will never forget Brigid or her cat. She made sure of that."

Stanley looked up at me. "Trent said Brigid hated cats. I don't understand."

Nemea's hands flew to her chest in a protective manner. "Is Brigid here? Is that who you want to talk about?"

"It is," I said. "But she's not here. She's gone missing. And so have two other witches called Avalon and Edie."

Nemea wavered on her feet. Her voice was so quiet that I could barely hear her words. "I hoped I would never hear those names again."

She looked as if she were going to faint, so I moved to her side and put a steadying hand on her arm. "Are you okay? Can I do something?"

She smiled sadly. "You could leave this place and never come back. But I can see the questions in your eyes. You won't leave until you get answers."

"It would really help us if we could talk," I said. "But I don't want to put your health at risk."

She patted my hand. "Thank you. But I'm stronger than I look. I don't want to talk about this in the open, not with everyone looking at us. Come to my house." She moved over to the tree Stanley had just climbed and pulled out a rope ladder. She swiftly made her way up the rungs.

Stanley whispered, "I can't see anyone watching us, but I can feel them."

"Me too." I shot a nervous look around us before following Nemea up the rope ladder. Stanley was up it in a flash. I wasn't, and by the time I got to the tree house platform, I was huffing and puffing.

Nemea took us into her little wooden house and invited us to sit at a table in the compact living area. She then brought us welcome drinks of cool water.

She began. "Brigid and those other witches lived here years ago. They just turned up one day and declared this as their home. Anyone who disagreed mysteriously disappeared. Brigid used terrible spells on others to get them to work for her. It was an awful time. A truly awful time."

An anger was growing in me over Brigid's behaviour.

Nemea's hands shook as she recalled the past. She clasped them tightly together. "Brigid always knew what was going on because of Edward. His fur was as black as night, and he would creep up on you without you seeing him. When the witches first arrived, we wanted to make them leave. We tried to make plans. But Edward knew about our plans. He must have been following us all the time. He told Brigid what we were planning. We couldn't talk freely with him lurking everywhere. But it was worse after he died and came back to life."

I spluttered on my drink. "Pardon? He died and came back to life?"

Nemea nodded. "He was old. The first time he died was because of his age. Brigid was distraught and brought him back to life. I heard the other witches arguing with her about that. They said it wasn't right. But she did it anyway. And Edward came back stronger and with more energy."

I stole a glance at Stanley. He was staring intently at Nemea.

"How many times was he brought back to life?" I asked.

Nemea shrugged. "Four or five, I think. It wasn't age which killed him the other times. It was his own recklessness. He thought he was invincible and took risks. Brigid always brought him back from the dead." She stopped talking for a moment. "But the final time he died was the worst. He was beyond resurrection. Brigid was so angry. I've never seen anyone like that before. She looked like she was going to explode with rage."

"What happened?" I asked.

"Someone trampled all over him," Nemea answered. "They squashed him. His body was broken. Brigid couldn't fix him. She tried. Over and over again. She forced the other witches to try too."

Stanley finally spoke, "Who trampled him?"

Nemea shrugged. "Someone on a horse. But we don't know who. Or whether it was done on purpose. But I do know that the other witch, Avalon, was to blame somehow. And I had seen her riding on a horse a few times. I heard Brigid shouting at her and saying it was all her fault, and that her careless ways had caught up with her. Avalon yelled back saying it wasn't her fault.

"Edward never came back to life. The witches left the next day and have never been back. But Brigid did something to us before she left. She cast a spell on our memories to make sure we remembered every evil thing she did here." She winced. "I try to forget, and when I sleep, the memories fade. But as soon as I wake up, they come back and I'm frightened all over again."

I pressed my lips together and tried to control the rage inside me. Brigid and the others would answer for their crimes.

Stanley said gently, "Cassia could do something about that spell. She can take it away." He looked at me hopefully. "Can't you?"

Nemea said, "Please, don't. I have other memories which come back to me every day. And I don't want those to go." A smile came to her face. "I have lovely memories about my sister. She was older than me. I loved her so much. I remember her face, and her laugh. I don't want to forget her."

I stiffened. "Where did she go?"

Nemea frowned. "I don't know. She left at the same time as the witches, but I don't know where she's gone. I miss her so much."

I braced myself for my next question. "What's her name?"

Nemea smiled. "Mirella." Then her smile died. "Why did she leave without saying goodbye? I wonder every day if she's even still alive."

Chapter 27

We said goodbye to Nemea and flew away.

As we left the small village behind us, Stanley said, "Why didn't you tell her about Mirella and that she's still alive? We could have collected Mirella and brought her here."

"I was tempted to tell Nemea about her sister, but Mirella is connected to the witches somehow. It could put Mirella's life in danger if we brought her here. Or that of her sister and the other woodland nymphs. If Brigid and the others are still alive, I don't want to lead them here. Not after what they did last time."

Stanley shuddered. "I don't like those witches at all. And if that cat were still alive I wouldn't like him either."

"Brigid must have put some of her cat-reviving magic in those blue flowers. But why?" I concentrated on the view ahead. I knew what I had to do next, but Stanley wouldn't like it.

We flew over the retirement village and towards the cottage where Mirella lived. I landed outside her front door. I got off the broomstick and was startled at the intense look Stanley was giving me.

He said, "You're going to use that dangerous spell on Mirella, aren't you? The one where you look into her memories. Cassia, you can't do that. It's not safe for you."

"I used it on you, at your request," I reminded him.

"But Mirella is full of sadness and pain. She'll pass it on to you. You might start screaming too. I won't let you do it." He stamped his paw. "I'm putting my paw down."

"Stanley, I have to do this. I have to find out what happened sixty years ago. And once I do, I might be able to help Mirella with her heartbreak. And if it helps me find those witches, I'll be able to bring them to justice. Don't you want that?"

He wasn't convinced. "What if they're dead?"

"Then I'll find out who killed them. If they are dead, it'll be safe to return Mirella to her sister. It's a win-win situation."

"No! It isn't!" he argued. "You know it isn't."

At that moment, Chifia came racing towards us. "What are you doing back? I saw you on your broomstick heading this way. I told you to leave Mirella alone! Don't you dare talk to her."

"I'm not going to talk to her," I explained calmly. "I'm merely going to delve into her memories."

Chifia screeched, "That's even worse! Why would you do such a thing? What's wrong with you?"

I briefly told her what I'd found out since I last saw her, including meeting Mirella's sister.

Chifia paled. "She has a sister? And they haven't seen each other for that long? That is so sad. Cassia, you have to do something to help them. Go into her memories, if that's what it takes."

"No!" Stanley cried out. "It's a dangerous spell. Cassia could absorb all of Mirella's pain and hurt. She might never recover. She could even die!"

"Is that true?" Chifia asked me.

"There's a very small chance I could get hurt. But I've done this spell before, and I've been fine." I gave her a bright smile.

Stanley padded over to me. "That's not true. You almost died on another case."

"But I didn't die." I crouched next to him. "I have to do this. It's the only way. Don't you want to help Mirella and Nemea?"

He looked away. "Yes, but I don't want you to get hurt."

I turned his chin so he was looking at me. "I won't. But if I do, send a message to Blythe and get help."

He opened his mouth to argue, but I gently closed it and said, "I'm doing this." I straightened up, looked at Chifia and asked, "Is Mirella inside?"

"She is. She's still asleep. Do you want me to wake her up?" Chifia grimaced. "She'll start screaming if I do that."

"No. It'll be better if she stays asleep." I felt Stanley leaning on my legs. He looked up at me with pleading eyes. "Stanley, come with me inside. Chifia, I'd like you there too. If I appear to be in danger, could you do something?"

"Like slap you around the face? Or throw a bucket of water over you? Yes, I can do that." She hitched her dress up and marched up to the front door. "Let's get on with it." She opened the door and went inside.

I followed her with Stanley still leaning against me as I walked along.

Mirella was lying in the middle of a large bed. Two female satyrs were sitting on chairs on either side of her. Mirella had a small smile on her face as if she was having a wonderful dream. I sighed. I was about to ruin her peace.

Chifia quickly explained to the satyrs what I was going to do. She tapped one of them on the shoulder and said, "Get a big bucket of water in case we need to throw it on the witch." The satyr looked shocked but she rushed out of the house.

I settled on the bed next to Mirella and held her hand in mine. Stanley went to her other side and fixed me with his eyes. I did feel sorry for him. I would feel just as anxious if he were doing this. Chifia sat on the chair next to Stanley and absent-mindedly stroked his head.

I cleared my mind and cast the spell.

Then I waited.

But not for long.

Mirella's memories came shooting at me from all directions.

Strong, fresh memories which twisted at my heart. They were coming at me too quickly to make any sense of them.

But I felt the wretchedness of them. Sadness didn't just gently wash over me; it flooded me. I felt like I was drowning in sorrow.

Down and down I went with the heavy despair.

The memories slowed down. I began to see them more clearly.

An image of Avalon's face appeared. She was close. Too close. Her face twisted in anger. She was shouting, "Keep away from him! He's mine!"

I felt fear over her words, but determination too. She wasn't going to tell me what to do.

Then a new memory.

Blue. Flecks of gold and silver.

A rush of immense love. Strong love.

The blue again. Blue eyes. Beautiful blue eyes with gold and silver flecks. He smiled at me. His eyes reflected the love I have for him. Our love is so strong.

Abruptly, Avalon's face is back. Her eyes were full of fury. "I warned you! And now look what you've done. He's dead! Because of you! You will pay for this."

The pain returned with a vengeance. Fresh pain. Clutching and squeezing my heart. I couldn't breathe with the pain.

Those blue eyes again.

Gone.

Oh, the pain! Why won't it go? Here it comes again.

I felt someone squeezing my hand. I opened my eyes and turned my head.

Mirella was looking at me. She said, "You felt it. My pain. It won't go away. It never goes away."

"I'm so sorry," I said with a lump in my throat. "Who was he? The one with blue eyes?"

A tear trickled down her cheek. "I can't remember his name. All I can remember are his eyes, and the love we had. Avalon said he was dead. She said it was my fault, and I should never have got in her way. She loved him too, but I don't think he loved her. She said he's dead, but he's still alive to me. He's never left my heart." More tears flowed.

I leaned over and brushed her tears away. "Can you remember what else Avalon said to you?"

"She wanted me to never forget about him. A spell was cast on me to make sure I would never forget how much I loved him, whoever he was. Avalon said I would stay the same age forever, and I would never recover from the loss of losing him. No matter how many years pass. My grief is fresh every day."

I heard sniffing coming from behind her. I raised my head to see Stanley and Chifia crying.

I helped Mirella into a sitting position and said, "I lost my mum when I was young. When the feeling of grief comes back to me, I make a mental list of all the lovely memories I have of her. It doesn't make the grief disappear, but it does lessen it." I wiped more tears from her cheeks. "I know it's going to be very hard with you having new grief every day, but can you concentrate just on the love you had? From what I experienced, he had a huge amount of love for you. And what lovely eyes he had! So beautiful."

She gave me a small smile. "I know. And I do like how he looked at me. Like I was the most important being in the world." She reached forward and wiped some of my tears away. "Those flowers you showed me look like his eyes."

I nodded. "They look exactly like his eyes. Brigid brought them to the retirement village. And she named them after you."

Mirella frowned. "Brigid? Do you mean Brigid Sangrey? The witch?"

I nodded.

"I've met her. It was years ago in the village where I grew up. Why did she make those blue flowers?" Mirella said with a frown.

"I really don't know. But I'm going to find out." I looked over at Stanley before continuing. "Do you remember anything about the village where you grew up?"

"Vaguely. The memories are fading. I do know that's where I met him, the one with blue eyes. And I remember the witches being there. They were so evil. I can still remember every bad thing they did." She shuddered. "Are they living in that retirement village you mentioned?"

I nodded again. "They were, but they've disappeared. Have you considered going back to your village?"

"I have, but I know my memories will make me start screaming again. It wouldn't be fair to the other nymphs to hear my terrible noise. I'm aware of my screams, but I can't control them. I don't know how the kind satyrs put up with me."

Chifia said, "We put up with you because we love you. Even when you're making that awful din."

I said to Mirella, "Stanley and I have just returned from your village. We talked to your sister. She misses you. Do you remember her?"

Mirella blinked rapidly. "I do. I miss her too. But I can't go back there. Ever."

"Mirella, do you know about Edward?" I asked.

I was surprised to see hate flash in her eyes. "That cat! He's evil through and through. He followed me everywhere I went. And not just me. He followed everyone. He was always spying on us. Horrible creature."

"He's dead," I said.

"Oh? Again? Brigid will bring him back to life. She was always doing that."

"Not this time," Stanley said. "He was squashed by a horse."

Mirella frowned. "A horse? Only one creature in my village owned a horse at that time. And that was Avalon. Did she kill Edward?"

I replied, "I don't know. But I know Brigid and Avalon had a fall-out over something." I got off the bed and stood with my hands on my hips. "I don't know what to make of this."

"What part?" Stanley asked me.

"All of it," I answered. "The witches have a corrupt past which may have caught up with them. But they've caused problems in the retirement village too, particularly with the wizards. The witches are missing, and they could be dead."

"They could be dead? Good. I'm glad," Mirella said. Her shoulders sagged. "I'm very sorry. That was mean of me."

Stanley put his paw over Mirella's hand. "I know I shouldn't say this, but I feel the same. They've done some terrible things."

The door was flung open causing us all to jump. The shorts-wearing satyr rushed in and straight over to my side. He grabbed my hand. "Cassia, my love! I've found you."

Chifia yelled at him, "Vrathix! Get your hands off her! We've talked about this."

Vrathix kept hold of my hand. "But I come with a message. Cassia, you're needed in the retirement village immediately." He gazed into my eyes. "And not just by me."

I pulled my hand free. "Why am I needed?"

"The witch is there, and threatening to kill everyone." He attempted to grab my hand again, but I was too quick for him.

I said, "Which witch?"

"That skinny one in a jumper. The one who was with you yesterday."

"Trent? Are you sure?"

"I am, my beautiful human. He's casting spells all over the place. He's injured two wizards."

Stanley was already racing out of the door. After a rushed goodbye, I went after him.

What was Trent up to now?

Chapter 28

Vrathix led us away from Mirella's cottage, through the forest and into the back area of The Fun Zone. He kept trying to hold my hand, but I made sure I kept my hands out of reach.

We heard Trent before we saw him. He was yelling about everything being a bunch of lies. Following the sound of his voice, we found him standing in front of a line of food carts. Two of the carts were on their sides with their contents spilling over the path. A couple of wizards were sitting on the grass. One was Arestrum The Great. He held a handkerchief to his bloodied nose. The other was Meevan The Marvellous. A huge bruise had blossomed on his cheek.

Trent's face was red with anger. Sparks of blue magic came from his fingers as he waved them madly around. He shouted, "You're all liars! My grandma would never hurt you. You're just jealous of her!"

The residents in front of him cowered in fear. They seemed unable to turn away. Had Trent cast a spell on them?

I'd seen enough. I shot magic over Trent and magical ropes appeared around him. I aimed extra magic at his dangerous hands and enchanted gloves soon covered them. He wouldn't be able to use magic now. He opened his mouth to yell at me, but I wasn't having any of that. A swift wave of my hand ensured his mouth stayed close.

I turned to the crowd and released them from any magic which was holding them in place. I said to them, "I'm so sorry this has happened. Is anybody hurt?"

There was mumbling and muttering. They shook their heads. Some of them began to run away.

A wide-eyed goblin came over to me and said, "Is this what it's going to be like now? Are we going to be terrorised by that witch over there? I thought Brigid was bad, but he's much worse."

"You're not going to be terrorised by Trent." I gave him a reassuring smile. "Or anyone else. Would you ensure everyone goes back to their homes and stays there until I get everything sorted out, please? I don't want anyone to get hurt."

"It's a bit late for that." He gave a nod in the direction of the fallen wizards. "That witch hit them with a bolt of magic. It was frightening."

"I'll check on them. Let me know if anyone else is hurt."

He nodded and then went over to a group of elderly creatures and talked to them. They gave Trent worried looks before moving away.

Vrathix put a warm arm around my shoulder. "What do you want me to do with the trouble-causer? I can throw him out of the village. Just say the word and I'll do anything you want, my love."

I shrugged his arm off my shoulder. "I'll deal with Trent. Could you make sure everyone goes back to their homes?"

He bowed. "Anything for you. We'll meet again, my one true love." He smiled into my eyes. Then something caught his attention behind me. "Belinda! Is that you? I haven't seen you in years. You're looking just as beautiful as ever. Be careful with those eyes of yours or I could fall in love with you. Oops! Too late." Without giving me a second look, he moved away.

I looked over my shoulder and saw him gazing at an elf. She was blushing as she held her hand out to him. So much for me being his one true love. I was relieved about that as I had enough complications at the moment. I turned my attention back to the biggest one. Trent was firing malicious looks at me. I turned away from him.

Stanley was standing next to Arestrum and I heard Stanley say, "That looks nasty. Do you want Cassia to help you?"

Arestrum snapped, "I don't want any witches near me! Nothing but trouble, the lot of them."

Ignoring his protests, I crouched at the wizard's side and moved the blood-covered handkerchief away. I wiggled my fingers over his injury and the blood disappeared.

Arestrum gingerly touched his nose. "Thanks," he muttered quietly. He cleared his throat. "What are you going to do about that evil one over there? You are going to do something, aren't you? If you don't, then I will."

I straightened up and pulled him to his feet. "Leave him to me. Go to your home and stay there."

He smoothed down his cloak. "You can't tell me what to do."

I gave him a long look. He averted his gaze. I said calmly, "I am dealing with this situation. I will deal with it better if you leave here. Okay?"

He grumbled a bit but then walked away. I went over to Meevan and used healing magic on his purple face.

As I helped him up, a look of delight came over his face. "What an experience!" he declared. "I must write a song about this. Yes, I can feel the melody already."

He made to move away, but I caught his sleeve and asked, "Where's the other wizard?" I'd totally forgotten his name.

"Oh? Him? Yes." Meevan scratched his head. "He was never here. What rhymes with terrifying?"

I shook my head at him. "I haven't got time to talk about rhymes. Go to your home and stay there."

Meevan gave me an absent nod as he walked away, already lost in his latest song.

I checked the area for any other residents. Everyone had left. The rides around us fell silent as they stopped moving. I used magic on the toppled carts and put them upright. Using more magic, I cleaned the area of debris. I was aware of Trent watching my every move. Good. I wanted him to. Stanley had positioned himself at Trent's feet like a guard-cat.

Once I was satisfied everything was in order, I stood in front of Trent and just looked at him. I didn't know where to begin.

A sudden weariness settled over me. What an awful investigation this was turning out to be.

Stanley tapped my legs. I looked down at him. He said, "I'll deal with this. Pick me up, please."

I gave him a grateful smile and pulled him into my arms. I turned so that Stanley was looking directly at Trent.

Stanley whispered to me, "Can he hear us?"

I nodded.

"Good." Stanley turned back to Trent. And then he let him have the full wrath of his anger.

Chapter 29

I had no idea Stanley could be so forceful. And so angry. He laid into Trent about how irresponsible he'd been. And how his thoughtless and reckless behaviour had caused harm to the wizards, and his ill-considered use of magic had scared the elderly residents who had done nothing wrong to Trent.

Even though Trent was bound in ropes and couldn't move, he seemed to wither under the barrage of Stanley's harsh words. Even when tears of shame welled in Trent's eyes, Stanley didn't stop. He said Trent was too foolhardy, too hot-headed and far too impetuous to be a witch.

Stanley turned his head away from Trent and said coldly, "I am ashamed of you. So very ashamed."

Ouch. Even I winced at those words.

The tears were flowing freely down Trent's face now. My anger over his behaviour dissolved. He was young. He was hurt and confused by his grandma's disappearance. But he was still an idiot for acting so rashly.

Stanley leaned his head against my cheek and whispered. "I'm done. Was I too harsh?"

I stroked his head and whispered back, "A little. But it needed to be said." I put Stanley down, removed the restraints from Trent and said, "Explain yourself."

Trent sank to the ground and put his head in his hands. His muffled voice came to us. "I'm so sorry. So very sorry. I'm so ashamed. I don't know what got into me."

I sat at his side and gently moved his hands away from his face. "Tell me why you acted this way."

Stanley sat in front of Trent and said, "We're waiting."

Trent wiped his nose with the back of his hand and avoided looking at Stanley. He said to me, "It's Grandma's book. Blythe has worked out what Grandma wrote. I heard her telling Luca about it in her house. They didn't know I was listening. They thought I was at the café, but I came back to Blythe's house. I heard everything."

I asked carefully, "What did you hear?"

"Blythe said Grandma had tormented hundreds of beings over the years. She'd hurt them for the fun of it. She'd cast curses on anyone who angered her." He looked away from me. "Blythe said Grandma was evil. She said Grandma had used black magic and that she was going to be judged by the witch council." His voice caught in his throat. "Luca said Grandma might not be alive. Then Blythe said it would be better for her if she wasn't."

"I'm sorry you had to hear that," I told him.

Stanley moved closer to Trent. "I'm sorry you heard that too."

"I wish I hadn't," Trent said with a sad smile. "No one wants to know their grandma is an evil witch who is hated by hundreds. I didn't believe Blythe's words. I just couldn't accept them. I know my grandma. I know what she's really like. I thought everyone was lying. I couldn't see sense through my anger."

"And you came here to release that anger," I said. "You took it out on innocent beings. You hurt those wizards."

"They got in my way. They tried to stop me." He shook his head sadly. "I couldn't stop my rage. It was like someone else was inside me. I saw myself doing those awful things, but

I couldn't stop." His head dropped. "I'm an evil witch, just like Grandma."

I put my hand on his arm. "You're not evil. But you have to control your anger."

Stanley padded closer and put his paw on Trent's leg. "We can help you with that."

Trent's smile was wobbly as he looked at Stanley. "I don't deserve your help. Stanley, I've hurt you the most. You're ashamed of me. And so you should be. I've ruined our friendship. Don't be kind to me. I don't deserve it."

Stanley smiled at him. "I'll decide where my kindness goes. Let's forget this happened."

"No. I can't, and I won't," Trent said. "I have to take responsibility. And I have to accept the truth about Grandma. She's not who I thought she was." He stood up and looked around the deserted area. "I'm going to apologise to each and every resident in this village. I'll start with the wizards. There's no excuse for my behaviour, but I can say sorry."

I got up. "That's a good start. It might take you a while."

"I don't care. I don't want everyone to think I'm like Grandma." His skinny chest puffed out. "I have to do this."

A scuttling figure dashed along the end of the path. What was she doing here?

Stanley noticed her too because he gave me a knowing look and said, "Cassia, haven't you got somewhere to be? Trent, do you want me to come with you?"

Trent's eyes widened. "You'd do that?"

"Of course. I'm proud of you for wanting to apologise." Stanley grinned at him. "And I want to make sure your anger doesn't get the better of you again."

Trent gave him a smile in return. "Thanks. I'll feel better with you at my side. Would it be okay if I picked you up?"

"I would like that." Stanley held his front paws up. "While we're walking, you can talk about Brimstone, and who you met there."

Trent scooped Stanley up and they began to walk away. Trent said, "I went to the café a few times. The food there is so delicious. I can't get enough of it. And then I met..." His voice trailed away as they left me.

As soon as they'd gone, I got on my broomstick and took to the air. I spotted the scuttling figure rushing along the path to the residents' homes. And the cheeky thing spotted me too. She gave me a cheery wave as she rushed over to Brigid's house.

I landed outside the same house and walked around the side.

I found her sitting on a bench with her little gnome legs dangling. Her wicker basket was on her knee. Mrs Tarblast patted the area next to her. "Sit down."

I propped my broomstick up. "What are you doing here?"

"Well, that's a fine welcome."

I sat next to her. "Sorry. I've got a lot going on."

Her eyes twinkled. "I know. Blythe told me. She didn't tell me everything, though. You know what she's like. She keeps forgetting we're colleagues." She patted her pockets as if looking for something. Then she opened the basket and looked inside. "Oh, there it is. Right next to my cheese roll. Here you are." She gave me a sealed envelope.

I took it. "Who's this from?"

"Blythe. Though why she had to seal it, I don't know. It's not as if I'd look at a private message." She tutted. "Well then? What does it say?"

I opened it and read the contents. Mrs Tarblast moved so close to me that she was almost on my knee. I quickly scanned the letter and then closed it.

I said, "There's some information on a spell Brigid used. And Blythe's confirmed what I've already discovered. Brigid had a cat called Edward. And she used spells to bring him back to life when he died. He died quite a few times."

Mrs Tarblast's hand flew to her chest. "I didn't know she had a cat. She never mentioned him. She must have used black magic to bring him back to life. Isn't that illegal for you witches?"

"It's illegal for everyone. Even you." I gave her a searching look. "Have you ever used black magic?"

"Certainly not. And you'll never prove it." She shuffled away from me. "I wonder why Brigid never told me? I thought we were friends."

I turned the envelope over in my hands as I considered whether I should tell her what else Brigid had been keeping from her. She probably already knew some of it from Blythe.

Mrs Tarblast opened her basket again and took some wrapped items out. She placed one on my knee and said, "I've made you something to eat. I know what you're like when you get lost in a case. You forget to eat. I've made us a flask of tea too. And seeing as I was up early, I baked some scones and made some jam. You can have that after your sandwich."

Her kindness brought tears to my eyes. I quickly blinked them away. "Thank you. That's so kind. And I am hungry."

"Me too." She took a few more items out, shuffled along the bench a bit and placed the items down so that we had ourselves a little picnic.

She said, "I've brought something for Stanley. Where is he? How's he doing? I hope he's keeping out of trouble." She chuckled. "I do love that cat. He's got a way about him, hasn't he?"

I couldn't keep the tears in this time.

Mrs Tarblast noticed and took my wrapped sandwich away. Her tone was gentle as she said, "Don't cry on your sandwich. You'll make it soggy. Right then. Tell me everything. First of all, is Stanley okay?"

"He is now."

"Now? What happened to him? Is this all part of your investigation? Do I need to put my official jacket on?"

"No. But you might need a packet of tissues." I began to tell her everything. When I got to the bit about Stanley, she did dissolve into tears. But she quickly recovered.

When I'd finished talking, she gave me the sandwich back. "So, let me get this straight. Brigid is a black-hearted witch who's gained countless enemies over the years?"

I nodded and bit into the sandwich.

"And the wizards who live here hated her too?"

Another nod from me.

"Well, you can count them out as suspects. I've met them. They haven't got the intelligence or courage to go against an experienced witch like Brigid. That leaves the Mirella mystery. Avalon must have been after that chap with the blue eyes, but he was in love with Mirella. Avalon got her revenge, probably with Brigid's help. And Edie has been part of it too."

With my cheeks bulging with food, I gave her a nod. The sandwich really was delicious.

Mrs Tarblast pointed to a bunch of blue flowers in front of us. "And those flowers resembled the chap's eyes and they're made of tears? They could be Mirella's tears. She might go sleepwalking, looking for her lost love. Avalon's curse could have made her cry tears which turned into these flowers. They would remind Mirella even more of her lost love. That is cruel." She looked at me. "Cassia, don't stuff your face like that. You'll give yourself indigestion."

I swallowed the food. "These flowers could be Mirella's tears. But if she wandered around here on a night-time, wouldn't someone have seen her?"

"Oh! These could be Avalon's tears. If Brigid blamed her for Edward's death, then Brigid could have put a curse on Avalon to make sure she knew Brigid hadn't forgiven her."

"That's a good point." I looked at the scones. "Those look delicious."

"Help yourself." She fell silent and appeared to be mulling something over. "I think Edie has got something to do with this. It's not by chance that everyone forgets who she is. I think she's made herself forgettable on purpose. I've seen her sneak up on residents and listen to their private conversations for a good ten minutes before she slips away."

"You could have another good point. This scone is lovely. So light and tasty. And the jam complements it so well."

She smiled. "I get the berries from a fairy village on the way here." She gave my half-eaten scone a pointed look. "I'd better get some more on the way home. Is that your second scone?"

"You did tell me to help myself. Do the fairies know you take their berries?"

"Of course they do! I don't steal, Cassia. I always ask for permission. Just like I did with Brigid and these flowers when we first met ten years ago."

I lowered the scone. "Ten years ago?"

"Yes. That's when she and the others moved here. She'd been on the waiting list for about twenty years. That's what she told me anyway. She offered to put my name on the list, but I told her firmly I have no intention of retiring. I like my work."

I put the scone on a plate at my side. "But why would Brigid be on a waiting list if she owns this village?"

"She owns it? Well, I never! She kept that to herself, like a lot of things it seems." She frowned. "But it doesn't make sense, does it? About her being on a waiting list if she owns this village?"

"No. It doesn't." A thought was niggling at my brain. I opened Blythe's note and read it again. My thoughts became clearer, like I was putting the last pieces of a jigsaw puzzle together.

Mrs Tarblast waved a hand in front of my face. "Cassia. What's going on? You've got a funny look on your face. Is it indigestion? I did warn you."

"No, it's not that." I looked at her. "I think I know who's behind this mystery. Would you do something for me?"

Chapter 30

Once Mrs Tarblast had left for Brimstone, I took my time to go over all the facts of this case. Most of it made sense, but there were some gaps. And I knew who could fill in those gaps. And I had to confront them before they took more action.

I collected my broomstick and walked away from Brigid's house. I was aware of residents peeping out of their windows. I was glad they were inside as I wasn't sure how my confrontation was going to go.

The village was eerily quiet as I walked along the paths and towards the clubhouse. Even the birds were silent.

I found Creg sitting cross-legged in front of the witches' statues and staring at them intently. I quietly sat next to him. I was aware of his unique odour, but it didn't bother me anymore. I took in the two bumps on his head, his facial features and the hairs poking through his trousers. I couldn't see his feet, but I'd seen enough of him to realise he was a satyr. A satyr who had changed drastically over the years.

Without looking at me, he asked, "What did you do to them?"

"I put a protective spell on them. I wasn't sure it would do any good, but it has. Hasn't it?"

Still looking straight forward, he replied, "It has. Unfortunately. They should have shrunk more by now. I thought I must have got the spell wrong. But then I figured you must have done something to stop them from getting smaller. You were hanging around here enough."

"Are they still alive in there?"

"Yeah." He let out a heavy sigh. "I wanted to kill them. But I couldn't bring myself to do it. So I made them into these. They're frozen. That book in Brigid's hand isn't hers, it's one of mine. I put it there to make the statues look authentic." A smile came to his face. "It was Brigid who gave me the idea for freezing them. I heard her bragging about doing this to a couple of werewolves who she had argued with. She was talking to that useless grandson of hers about them. She even told him how to do the spell. It wasn't hard."

"What were you going to do with them?"

"Nothing. I liked seeing them getting smaller each day. Especially Brigid. She doesn't look so important now does she? I thought they'd get so small that they'd disappear into nothingness eventually." He turned his dark eyes on me. "You worked out my lie then?"

"The one about Brigid owning the village? Yes. It took me a while. You would only lie about that because you're the one who owns it. How long have you owned it? Sixty years?"

"Thereabouts. What else have you worked out?"

I pointed to the Mirella Phlox. "Those are your tears. You named them, and this village after Mirella."

His look softened. "Mirella. Yes. I think about her almost every second of every day. Brigid made sure of that. I tried to forget about Mirella and the love we had, but Brigid did something to me to make sure my pain is real every day. The only way to make it better is by crying. And, yes, my tears do turn into these flowers. Thanks to Brigid's spell."

I thought about the constant tears I'd been shedding over Stanley's accident. Creg must have cried thousands of tears, maybe millions. I said, "There are a lot of flowers."

"I'm in a lot of pain. I suppose you want to let these witches go free now. I bet you think they've done nothing wrong. You're just like them."

I replied, "I'm nothing like them. And I'm not going to release them, not yet. I want to know about you and Mirella. How did you meet?"

He smiled and seemed much younger. "I met her in the fields outside her village. She was singing to herself as she picked flowers. She was so beautiful. I fell in love with her the second I saw her. I just stood there, staring hopelessly at her. Then she looked at me. It was like an arrow piercing my heart. I knew I would never love another. She was made for me. And I was made for her."

"Did she feel the same?"

He laughed. "Yes. I couldn't believe my good fortune. This beautiful creature liked me. More than that; she loved me. We talked for hours. Well into the night. She told me witches had invaded her village but warned me not to get involved. She said they weren't good witches and could hurt me." His good mood evaporated. "But I had to do something. I hid away until I saw one of the witches leave the village one day. It was Avalon. I made myself known to her and told her about my concerns. She looked so friendly that I thought she'd understand. But she didn't. She said I was a fool to love a mere woodland nymph and would be better off with her. Of course, I turned her down. That was a mistake."

"I can't imagine many creatures turned Avalon down. She has lots of admirers."

Creg said, "I wasn't one of them. But Avalon pursued me. She said she loved me, and I would soon love her. I refused her over and over. I even heard her threatening Mirella one day. That was the last straw. I told Avalon I would never love someone like her. Never. That was another mistake."

"What did Avalon do?"

"She chased me on a horse one day. She came thundering out of the trees and straight at me. There was evil in her eyes. I ran away as quickly as I could, but I was no match for her. She was right behind me all the time, getting closer. She only stopped when she—" He stopped talking and ran a hand over the back of his neck. "I still feel sick at the memory of it."

"She killed Brigid's cat," I said. "She trampled him."

Creg nodded. "There was barely anything left of that cat. Avalon started screaming. She said it was all my fault. But then Brigid appeared. She was furious. She knew it was Avalon's fault. But Brigid turned on me and said I shouldn't have turned Avalon's head in the first place. Brigid did some magic so I couldn't move, and then she explained how she was going to get her revenge on me."

I shook my head. "But it was Avalon's fault. Why didn't she punish her?"

"That's a question I've asked myself for years. Maybe she got more pleasure from hurting innocent beings. Avalon said she would curse Mirella so she'd forget about me."

I knew that wasn't true, but I kept silent.

Creg continued. "That wasn't enough for Avalon. She said a curse would be put on my village so no one would remember me, ensuring that I could never go home. And she was going to plant a tale in the satyrs' heads about how mixing with other species would be a bad thing. I don't know if that worked."

"It did. I've been to your village. I met Chifia who gave me half a story about something terrible happening to a satyr years ago."

Creg gave me a small smile. "I grew up with Chifia, but she won't remember me because of Brigid's curse. I keep an eye on the village. It does make me cry but my tears don't turn into flowers there. I don't know why that is."

"And your tears don't turn into flowers when you watch over Mirella," I prompted.

His smile grew. "I didn't even know she was there until a few years ago. I noticed Chifia leaving the satyr village one day and decided to follow her out of curiosity. I couldn't believe it when I saw Mirella in that little cottage. She's still beautiful. She doesn't seem to have aged a day. I hope she's happy. I like her being close to my village. I keep my distance and make sure she never sees me. She doesn't remember me." He waved a hand over his face. "And she wouldn't like what I've become. I don't look anything like I used to. I've changed slowly over the years."

"That's because of Brigid's spell." I showed him the letter Blythe had sent me and explained how Blythe had decoded Brigid's spellbook. "It's a metamorphic one. It changed everything about you. Even your blue eyes. It's a truly evil spell. You didn't deserve it."

"Try telling Brigid that. She didn't care who she hurt."

I asked, "Why do you have satyrs working for you? They must remind you of how you once looked."

He shrugged. "They're the only ones who apply for the jobs. Maybe that's another part of the curse Brigid put on me. As if taking Mirella away from me wasn't enough. Although, some of the satyrs do give me funny looks sometimes, as if they know I'm one of them."

I said, "Why did you move here? So close to your village?"

"I wanted to be close to them. Nobody owned this land, so I built a small house where the clubhouse is. I thought I might as well do something with myself. I started making the grounds tidy. I soon had some nosy creatures turning up to see what I was doing with this land. They thought I could do with some help. I said I was fine on my own, but they wouldn't leave me alone. They started going on about how peaceful it was, and how interesting those blue flowers were. Interfering lot. I couldn't get rid of them no matter how hard I tried."

"I noticed The Forest Zone looks like Mirella's village. Was that your doing?"

He gave me a sideways look. "Yes. You do get around, don't you?"

"Why did you let the witches in?"

"I wasn't going to. But Brigid and Avalon kept turning up here pestering me." He paused as he looked back at the stone figures. "They didn't remember me. And they certainly didn't remember what they'd done to me."

I pointed to Edie. "But she knew who you were, didn't she?"

He gave me a direct look. "She's the worst of them. Let me tell you what she did."

Chapter 31

Creg continued talking. "When I first met Mirella, she pointed out the witches to me, from a distance, of course. Not long after, Edie started turning up in peculiar places. Whenever I met up with Mirella, I'd spot Edie walking through the trees not far away. She would acknowledge us with a knowing smile. Even when Mirella and I agreed to meet in areas far from Mirella's village, that witch would never be far away. I think she must have used magic to keep turning up like that."

I nodded. "I've heard that about her over and over again."

"She was there when Avalon killed Edward, hiding in the bushes. But she didn't tell Brigid the truth. She walked out as if she'd just been passing by. She agreed with Brigid that I was to blame and should be punished. Brigid did so, and wrote the spells down in that book she always carried. Then Edie said Brigid should cast a spell on herself so she'd forget about Edward, his death and me."

I frowned. "Why would she need to do that?"

"Edie argued it would be too painful for Brigid to think about Edward, and if she ever met me again, that would bring painful memories up for Brigid."

I let out a cry of outrage. "But that's exactly what Brigid did to you! She made sure your painful memories came up every day."

"I know. But Brigid didn't care. She let Edie cast the forgetting spells. And Edie sneakily cast one on Avalon too. She also put an extra one on Brigid to convince her that cats were not to be trusted. I think Edie had hated Brigid's cat for years and didn't want another one coming along. Then Edie tore a page from Brigid's book and waved it in my face. She said, "There's no going back for you." She destroyed the page right in front of me."

I shook my head. I was at a loss for words.

But not for long. After a few seconds, I asked, "Did Edie recognise you when they came here?"

He nodded. "Not at first. My appearance had become worse over the years. I no longer looked anything like a satyr. I had more hairs. More boils. My smell increased. I even changed my name. Most creatures try to avoid looking at me. But Edie was soon up to her old ways and began to sneak up on me. She must have had an inkling that she knew me. And she'd noticed there were more blue flowers around the witches' homes than anywhere else. The tears I shed there were full of hate."

I nodded in understanding.

Creg continued. "Edie followed me to Mirella's home one day. I didn't know about that until I returned home and she confronted me." He stared at Edie's stone figure. "That's when the torments and extortion began. I had to do her bidding, over and over again. And that of the other witches too. They got away with terrible behaviour, especially Brigid. Edie loved the damage Brigid caused. She said if I did anything to stop it, then she'd bring Brigid's memories back. And Brigid would delight in delivering more curses, not just on me, but on everyone who lived here. I couldn't let that happen."

I looked at Edie. So quiet and meek looking. Yet so devious and calculating.

Creg muttered, "I'm sorry for what I did to your cat."

"You were the one on the flying carpet?"

"I was. I didn't mean to cause any harm. I wanted to keep an eye on Brigid's grandson. I thought he might be as evil as her."

"Did you fly into them on purpose?" I don't know how I managed to keep my voice calm, but I did.

"No. It was Trent who flew at me. He was useless at flying and that carpet wasn't flying in a straight line. But I shouldn't have been so close. I can't tell you how sorry I am about that cat of yours."

"He's okay now," I said curtly. "Did you follow me in The Fun Zone when I was near the nightclubs?"

"I did. I wanted to keep an eye on you. I didn't want you to find out what I'd done."

I sighed. "I don't agree with what you've done, but I can understand why you did it. I can undo the metamorphic spell on you. I'm not sure about the memory one, but I could ask Blythe for help on that."

"What's the point? I've lived like this for years. Anyway, Mirella's forgotten about me. Looking like I used to do, and knowing she didn't love me, would only cause me more heartache."

This was the perfect time to tell him about Mirella and her dreams about him. But I didn't get the chance because Stanley came rushing over to me.

He put his paws on my knees and asked urgently, "Cassia, what do you call a sky full of witches?"

"Stanley, I haven't got time for riddles."

"This isn't a riddle. It's a question. Look." He gazed upwards.

I did so too. I felt my mouth drop open.

The sky was full of witches. All on broomsticks. All heading our way. There must have been hundreds of them. As they came closer, I could see how different they were. Some were clad in shorts and T-shirts; others wore long dresses encrusted with jewels. I spotted a few in bikinis. The one who waved to me was wearing a long purple dress.

Stanley waved at her. "Blythe! Hi!"

The witches at the front descended and lowered themselves silently on the grass behind the statues.

Blythe got off her broomstick, gave me a nod and said, "You can release them now."

I stood up and aimed my hands at the frozen witches. I paused. "Stanley, go and stand next to Blythe. These three are going to be furious when they come out of the spell."

He stood squarely in front of me. "I'm not going anywhere."

Creg got to his feet and declared, "Me neither. I'm ready for them."

"I'm not sure I am," I muttered. Bracing myself, I aimed magic at Brigid, Avalon and Edie.

The statues grew. Then they cracked open to reveal the living witches inside.

The silence was pierced by a cacophony of noise. Shrieks, screams, wails and threats hurled our way. The three witches were incandescent with rage and pushed each other out of the way to get to us. I'd already put a magical safety barrier in front of us, so they didn't get very far.

Brigid pounded on the invisible barrier and screamed, "Let us through! You will pay for this! I will rip your head off! I will snap you in two! I will—" Her threats were silenced as Trent appeared at my side. The anger fled from Brigid's face. "Trent? What are you doing here? Don't listen to anything these liars say. They're jealous of my talent."

Trent held his hands up. "Grandma, I know everything. Everything." His head dropped. "I can't look at you."

Edie pointed at Creg. "It's his fault, Brigid! He's the one who should be punished! Do it! Do it now."

There was a strange tapping noise behind them which caused the three witches to stop moving. It took me a moment to work out what the noise was.

Then I saw them. The witches on the ground and in the air. They were all tapping slowly on their broomsticks. The grave looks on their faces made me shiver.

I don't know what the tapping signified, but it had a strong effect on Brigid, Avalon and Edie. They turned around, fell to their knees and pleaded with the witches to stop.

Blythe held her hand up and the noise ceased. She walked up to the three witches and said, "You will answer for every single one of your crimes. Now, leave." She clicked her fingers and a black mist enveloped the witches. It swirled around them like a tornado and lifted them towards the waiting witches in the sky. The waiting witches circled the tornado. They each held a single hand towards it, and then they flew away taking the tornado with them.

"Wow," Stanley said. "That was amazing."

Blythe came over to us. She addressed Creg, "I can't even begin to apologise for what those witches did to you. But I can undo the spells which were cast on you and others." She glanced at me. "Mrs Tarblast has told me everything."

"Don't bother with me," Creg told Blythe. "I am who I am."

Blythe raised one eyebrow at him. "Fair enough. But I won't let others suffer." She clapped her hands, turned slowly around and mumbled one strange word after another.

There was a slight shift in the air. I waited for something to happen, but nothing changed. And Creg looked the same.

Trent said to Blythe, "Can I have Grandma's book, please?"

"Why?" she asked.

"I want to visit those beings she's upset and try to make things right. And if I can't do that, I want to at least apologise for her."

Blythe gave him the book. "That is commendable of you, but it will take years and years."

He shrugged. "I'm young." He looked at the first page. "Oh! I can read it."

"I got rid of the codes," Blythe said with a smile. "And I've removed details of the spells. They were too horrific to look at. Only the names and addresses of the victims and their families remain."

Trent nodded. "That's all I need. Thank you." He turned to me. "And thank you, Cassia, for getting to the truth."

"I had a lot of help," I told him.

Trent crouched in front of Stanley. "I'm so glad we met. And I'm sorry I was awful to you when we first did meet."

"I've already forgotten that part. Trent, don't spend all your time apologising for your grandma."

"I have to. It feels like something I should do." He stroked Stanley's head. "But if I'm near Brimstone, can I call in to see you?"

"Absolutely!" Stanley said with a grin.

Trent straightened up and faced Blythe. He said, "I'd better get going. What will happen to Grandma?"

"She'll atone for her crimes."

"Will you hurt her?"

Blythe shook her head. "Witch justice doesn't involve pain. A bit of discomfort now and again, but not pain. Trent, you're not alone. Look at my fellow witches behind me. They've come from all over the lands. They will help you on your quest of apology. It won't take as long as you think."

He looked towards the witches. "They'll help me?"

"They will. And I've brought someone else to help you. A witch needs a familiar." She clicked her fingers and a fluffy ginger cat sauntered out from the group of witches. Blythe lowered her voice, "Angelica is an experienced familiar, but she has a bit of an attitude."

Angelica came right up to Trent and sniffed him. She declared, "We'll start with personal hygiene, young witch. Bathing twice a week will not do. And what is going on with your hair? Did a family of birds make a nest in it? And don't get me started on what you're wearing." She looked him up and down, turned around and ordered, "Follow me. We can work together. But I'm in charge for now."

Trent beamed at Stanley and me. He said, "I love her!" He ran after Angelica.

Before any further talking could proceed, a vision in a long dress shot towards us. She screamed at Creg, "You! Qealwaun! It's you! I would know you anywhere!"

"Mirella?" Creg's voice was barely audible. "You remember me?"

She flung herself at him and wrapped her arms tightly around his neck. She smiled into his eyes. "You look a bit different, but my heart knows you." She planted kiss after kiss on his surprised face.

Creg, or Qealwaun, slowly smiled and gazed at Mirella. The slightest hint of blue came to his eyes.

Mirella paused in her kisses and said, "You have to meet my sister. Right now. Come on. And we need to plan our future. I am never letting you out of my sight!"

More blue came to the satyr's eyes. He gently took Mirella's hand in his and they walked away, eyes locked on each other.

Blythe took Stanley and me to one side. She said, "You two can go home. I'll deal with everything here. I know what needs to be done." She picked Stanley up and handed him to me. "Don't for a minute think black magic has got anything to do with Stanley's resurrection. It was a mixture of your love and magic, and Creg's love in those flowers which caused Stanley to come back. And he's going to be around for longer than most familiars."

"I'm glad," was all I could mutter.

Stanley rested his head against my chest. "Let's go, Cassia. I need a nap. All this being young has worn me out." He lifted his head. "Are you okay with me being around for much longer than most familiars?"

I tutted. "As if you need to ask me! Let's go." I gave him an extra long hug before we got on my broomstick and flew away from the Mirella Retirement Village, so thankful that this investigation was over.

And knowing that we'd be dealing with another one soon.

About the author

I live in a county called Yorkshire, England with my family. This area is known for its paranormal activity and haunted dwellings. I love all things supernatural and think there is more to this life than can be seen with our eyes.

I hope you enjoyed this story. If you did, I'd love it if you could post a small review. Reviews really help authors to sell more books. Thank you!

This story has been checked for errors by myself and my team. If you spot anything we've missed, you can let us know by emailing us at: april@aprilfernsby.com

You can visit my website and sign up to my newsletter at: www.aprilfernsby.com[1]

Many thanks to Paula for her proofreading work: Paula Proofreader[2]

Warm wishes

April Fernsby

---

1. http://www.aprilfernsby.com
2. https://paulaproofreader.wixsite.com/home

The Brimstone Witch Mysteries:

Book 1 - Murder Of A Werewolf

Book 2 - As Dead As A Vampire

Book 3 - The Centaur's Last Breath

Book 4 - The Sleeping Goblin

Book 5 - The Silent Banshee

Book 6 - The Murdered Mermaid

Book 7 - The End Of The Yeti

Book 8 - Death Of A Rainbow Nymph

Book 9 - The Witch Is Dead

Book 10 - A Deal With The Grim Reaper

Book 11 - A Grotesque Murder

Book 12 - The Missing Unicorn

Book 13 - The Satyr's Secret

The Psychic Café Series

Book 1 - A Deadly Delivery

Book 2 - A Fatal Wedding

Book 3 - Tea And Murder

Book 4 - The Knitting Pattern Mystery

Book 5 - The Cross Stitch Puzzle

Sign up to my newsletter here: www.aprilfernsby.com[3]

Follow me on Bookbub[4]

---

3. http://www.aprilfernsby.com

4. https://www.bookbub.com/authors/april-fernsby

The Satyr's Secret
A Brimstone Witch Mystery
(Book 13)
By
April Fernsby
www.aprilfernsby.com

Made in the USA
Las Vegas, NV
12 September 2021